DRUMS of WAR

Originally published
as *Broken Drum*

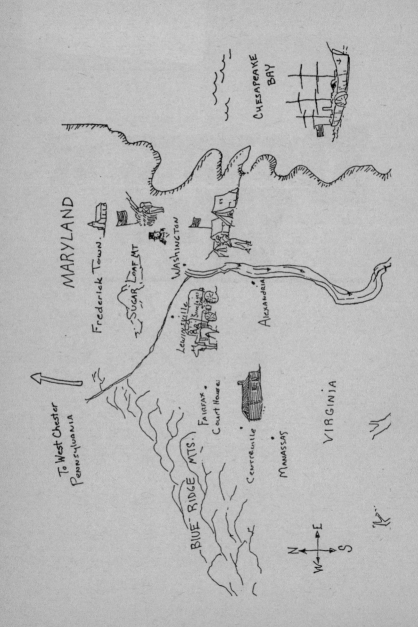

To West Chester
Pennsylvania

MARYLAND

Frederick Town

SUGAR LOAF MT.

Washington

CHESAPEAKE BAY

Lewinsville

Alexandria

BLUE RIDGE MTS.

Fairfax Court House

Centreville

Manassas

VIRGINIA

N
W — E
S

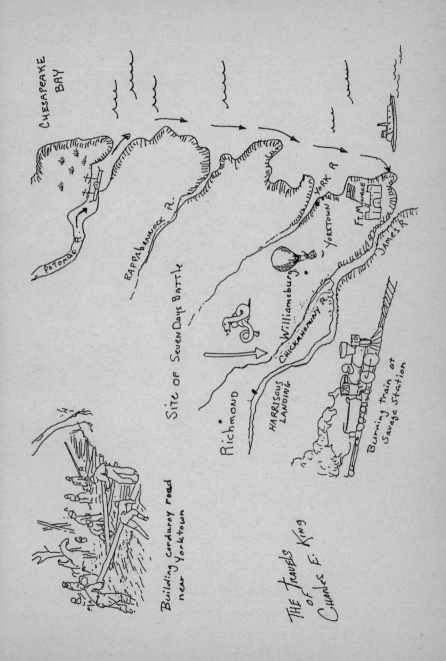

CHESAPEAKE BAY

POTOMAC R.

RAPPAHANNOCK R.

Site of Seven Days Battle

Richmond

Williamsburg

YORKTOWN

YORK R.

CHICKAHOMINY R.

HARRISON'S LANDING

JAMES R.

Ft. MONROE

Building corduroy road near Yorktown

Burning train at Savage Station

THE Travels of Charles E. King

DRUMS of WAR

Originally published as *Broken Drum*

Charles E. King

DRUMS of WAR

Originally published
as *Broken Drum*

By
Edith Morris Hemingway
and
Jacqueline Cosgrove Shields

Map and Illustrations by
Kenneth L. Cosgrove

SCHOLASTIC INC.
New York Toronto London Auckland Sydney
Mexico City New Delhi Hong Kong Buenos Aires

Charley King was an actual drummer boy in the Pennsylvania 49th Volunteers and did participate in the defense of Washington, the Peninsula Campaign, and the Battle of Antietam. However, many of the events and other characters are products of the authors' imaginations.

Originally published as *Broken Drum*

ISBN 0-439-91441-8

12 11 10 9 8 7 6 5 4 3 2   6 7 8 9 10 11/0

Printed in the U.S.A.   40

First Scholastic printing, September 2006

Dedicated to our husbands
Douglas Hemingway and Alexander Shields
and to our children
Daniel and Katie Hemingway
and
Katherine, Elizabeth, and Alec Shields
With our love

We harken back
to days of yore
and tell of the glory
that is war.
We sing the songs,
but hear not the
moan
of all the dead
who died
alone.

J.C.S.

Contents

CONTENTS

Chapter One

Lewinsville, Virginia —— September, 1861

The rain dripping on the canvas of the tent beat out a tat-too—hard, soft, soft, soft, hard, soft, soft, soft. Charley kept the rhythm with his fingers. For as long as he could remember, he had felt the rhythm in everything; even the way the wind blew through the big chestnut tree outside his bedroom window and moved the branches so they swayed up and down, side to side, casting shadows on the wall across from his bed, like dancers in a musicless dance. But Charley could hear the music and feel that erratic rhythm. One night when he was only eight years old, he realized that other people did not feel and hear as he did. That night he beat out the rhythm of the silent leaf dance on the foot board of his bed with two wooden spoons appropriated from Mama's kitchen. Papa came into the room and demanded, "What's all the infernal noise?" He knew then that Papa and others could not see the invisible dance or feel its rhythm.

Only Grandpa Eb could feel the music as he did. Old Eb-enezer Holt would step lively down the streets of West Chester, Pennsylvania with young Charley striding along beside him, both keeping time to silent music. Charley smiled as he remembered.

He could hear Grandpa Eb telling the story as clearly as if he were right there in the tent with him.

"Yes, sir, we marched down side of the old Mississip, drum beating a slow march. Then I got the order from Old Hickory, Andy Jackson hisself, 'Boy . . . play double time . . . quick march.' And we played, Old Betsy and me, for the honor and glory of these United States, and we kept on playin'. We plowed clean through those red coats and sent them a runnin', yes sir. War of 18 and 12 it was."

Charley and Ebenezer would practice for hours with the hickory sticks on the old wooden table out in the shed. "Jest look at old Betsy. She's waitin' till you're ready," Eb would say, and Charley would look, eyes wide, at the weather beaten old drum hanging lopsided on the peg in the corner.

"Soon now, Grandpa? Will I be ready soon?"

"Now don't rush, son. You will know when you're ready and so will I. So will Betsy. She'll sing for you, so she will."

As Charley lay there thinking of home, he was thankful for Grandpa and all the hours of practice. When he had been ready to play Old Betsy, and Eb had reverently taken the drum from the peg and placed the strap around Charley's neck, he had seen how proudly his grandfather marched with him. They became a common sight on the streets of West Chester, the young boy and the old man marching. When Captain Sweeney, the recruiter for the Pennsylvania 49th Volunteers, saw the two-man parade and heard Charley play the "long roll," "tattoo," and "reveille," he knew he wanted Charley in his company.

"Young man, you will be part of the defense of our Union against the rebellious Confederate states and bring honor to your proud parents and the Pennsylvania 49th," said Captain Sweeney. "Why, twelve years old is practically a man. Do you want to stay at home with the younger children and miss out on this chance for glory?"

"Please, Papa. Oh please, Mama," Charley had begged his parents. Now thinking of home and feeling a bit homesick, Charley rolled over on his cot and closed his eyes. A sharp blow across the small of his back sent him sprawling out of his bunk onto the plank floor. In the dark, he struggled to get up, but was pushed down again by a boot on the side of his neck, pressing into his shoulder. He tried to see who it was, but it was too dark, and the pain was so strong that he could not concentrate. Gradually his eyes made out a tall form standing over him and the other boys gathered around.

"Think you're pretty smart, don't ya?" Frank Simpson said. Charley remembered him from earlier in the day when the drummer boys assembled. Simpson was the lead drummer, taller and older than most of the other boys. "Well, answer me, you little rat. Think you're pretty smart?"

"Yes . . . I mean no, no," Charley stammered. The boot on his neck was pressing harder now, and he was starting to feel lightheaded.

"Come on, Simpson, leave him be," someone said.

"Sure, sure, I'll leave him be, just as soon as he learns who is top drummer here. It don't make no difference if he can play Yankee Doodle all day long, I'm senior drummer in this regimental drum corps. Say it, smart-aleck, say I'm leader here, or I'll crush your windpipe."

"Yes . . . yes . . . you're leader," Charley whispered.

"Say it again," the figure looming over him repeated as Charley almost slipped into unconsciousness.

Someone pulled Simpson away. "Come on, Frank. Leave him be now, or you'll have us all in trouble."

The figures moved further into the darkness of the tent. Charley painfully lifted himself from the floor into his cot and braced himself for another possible assault. Eventually he slipped into sleep from exhaustion and pain.

Dawn was not yet breaking when the sound of a deep voice awakened him. "Have mercy," Sergeant O'Toole muttered as he lifted the lantern high above his head and peered into the dark tent at the motionless figures sprawled in different positions.

"Babes, the lot a' them. Nothing but babes. And I have ta make battle tough men a' them. Lord help me!

"All right, up and on your feet now, lads!" he bellowed. "Who do ya think's gonna drum this regiment inta assembly? That's your job!"

The forms came to life, some startled, some more slowly, but all moved and came to various stages of wakefulness. Charley moved to a sitting position and reached out for his uniform. He winced from the pain.

"What's this?" O'Toole said as the light of the lantern shone on Charley's bruised face and neck. "Who did this ta ya, boy?" His voice lowered. "Ya did not look like this last night."

Charley pulled himself to his feet and looked away from the sergeant and the glare of the lantern. "No one, Sergeant . . . I . . . I fell . . . going to the latrine, sir, I mean Sergeant."

O'Toole straightened and hung the lantern on the overhead hook. "Assembly in five minutes, on the parade ground," he barked. "At daybreak, reveille sounds!"

The twelve members of the regimental drum corps scrambled into parade position, some still buttoning their uniforms. Charley struggled with the weight of the drum pulling against his bruised neck and nearly stumbled when Frank Simpson gave him a shove from behind. He realized his right boot was still untied as Sergeant O'Toole called them to attention.

"Now listen ta me, lads. In two minutes ya will sound reveille and wake the camp. Then ya will beat roll call. Then ya will beat mess call. Then ya will beat sick call. Then ya will practice and drill and drill and practice until the arms want ta fall off of ya and the wind is blown out of ya. And then ya will practice some more." He came closer to the corps, bending his broad frame to eye level with Frank Simpson. O'Toole's red handlebar moustache quivered as he lowered his voice and spoke, as if he had been present when Frank bullied Charley. "I want no enemies here! The enemy is in the south! You are the tongue of the regiment in camp. You say when ta wake up, when ta assemble, when ta eat, when ta go ta sick call."

Louder now, he continued as he paced. "In battle, you are the heart of the regiment. When a fightin' man is lost in the haze and groans of the dyin', with shells screamin' overhead and bullets whizzin' past, with so much smoke that a man will not know if he's dead or alive, it is you with the steady beat a' the drum who will rally him and give him heart and direction ta go on."

Charley stood at attention as the first bugle call sounded at encampment headquarters, signaling the surrounding camps. Sergeant O'Toole straightened and turned. Walking to the front of the line, he commanded, "Buglers sound reveille!"

Charley joined in beating the drum with a roll increasing in volume until the sound was deafening. Men poured from the tents in various stages of dress and undress. Horses whinnied to be fed. McClellan's Army of the Potomac was alive and moving, a fierce giant awakened by the boys of the regimental drum corps.

The final drum beat sounded, and each soldier was in place for the first roll call of the day. Company F of the Pennsylvania 49th Volunteers stood at attention as Sergeant O'Toole shouted out their names.

Charley glanced sideways, putting a name to some of the faces of his tent companions. "Anderson!" O'Toole boomed. "Here," shouted the dark haired lad next to him. Charley knew him to be Jamie, the one in the tent who had shared the last of his homemade cakes with him. He was taller than Charley by a head and played the bugle as though he had been doing it all his life.

Henry Jones answered next, and Charley shuddered at the memory of his dirty blonde head and wide mouthed grin laughing along with Frank Simpson.

Charley was brought back to the present by his own name, "King." "Here," he answered.

Patrick Lynch answered in quick succession. Another friend of Frank Simpson, he was the fifer in the company. Then came Hans Schmidt, a large, lanky blonde from Pennsylvania Dutch

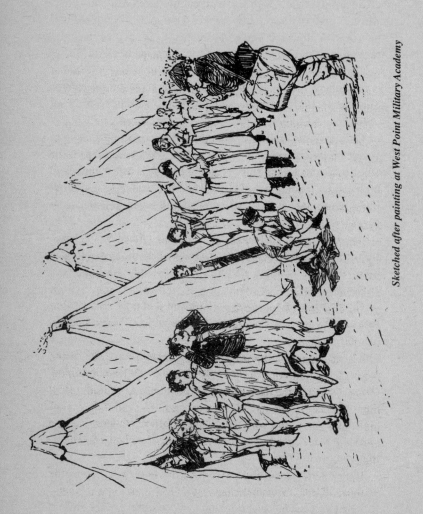

Sketched after painting at West Point Military Academy

country around Lancaster, who, like Charley, played the drum. He was a friendly type with a ready smile and laughing blue eyes.

From just over his left shoulder, Charley heard Frank Simpson's "here," and somehow that simple word held menace for him. He knew very well that Frank was here. The other names ran together in his mind until roll call was complete.

"Company diss-missed!" shouted Sergeant O'Toole, and the men wandered off to get ready for the rest of the day or roll back into blankets for an extra half hour's sleep.

"Here, not you, lads," O'Toole said. "You are ta help the cooks get the breakfast fires goin'. You and you," he said pointing at Charley and Patrick. "You two gather wood for the cook fires. Mind you don't wander far. We're in enemy territory on this side a' the Potomac, and even if the Rebs aren't around, some a' their sympathizers are not beyond shootin' at anythin' blue that moves."

As Charley and Patrick walked away from camp toward the creek, they eyed each other warily. Finally past the sentry, the boys stopped to look around. The smell of the fires drifted on the morning air. The mist rising from the water and the sounds of horses being curried and harnessed lent excitement to the atmosphere. The boys burst into a full run when Patrick called, "Race you!" to Charley. They ran stumbling and laughing down to the muddy bank.

Patrick picked up a branch of wood and held it to his shoulder, aiming it like a rifle. "Bang, Bang," he shouted, pointing it across the creek. "I'll bet those bushes are crawling with Johnny Rebs just waiting to get a shot at us. But I ain't scared, are you?"

"No, coz I don't think the Rebs are here yet."

"My ma and pa didn't want me to join up. How about yours?"

"Well, at first no. But Captain Sweeney visited my folks and promised I'd be safe as a drummer boy. And drumming is what

I aim to do for the honor of the Union." Charley bent to pick up wood and winced as a sharp pain ran down his arm.

"That from last night?" Patrick asked sympathetically. "Should be better soon."

"Yeah," said Charley as he shifted the wood to his other arm. The boys started back to camp, picking up kindling as they walked.

Patrick continued the conversation. "My pa says this here war is going to be over by Christmas."

"Do you really think we'll be home by Christmas?"

"Why sure, my pa's pretty smart, and if he says it's so, it's so."

Charley thought of the big tree in the front hall, the garlands over the windows, the excitement of his little brothers and sisters, and the food. Oh, the delicious food! "I sure do hope your pa is right," he said as he dropped the damp wood by the big cook fire.

"And just what am I to do with this lot?" shouted the corporal. "This stuff is wet! Do yuz want me to cook breakfast or smoke it?"

Charley and Patrick backed up, frightened by the fury in the voice of the company cook. He was a tall man with protruding teeth and a bald head. He stood up straight and pointed, shouting, "Go get me some DRY wood!"

The boys did not hesitate, but backed away as swiftly as they could and then turned and ran. When out of sight of the angry cook, they stopped and started to laugh, pointing at each other.

"Oh, you should have seen your face when he pointed at you," said Charley.

"My face?" said Patrick. "You were the one who scrambled like a crab backwards, when he stood up."

"Do you think he was scalped by Indians?"

"Could be, he sure is mean enough to live through that." This started another round of laughter. Presently the boys returned, this time with dry wood.

The boys of the drum corps were the first to rise, the last to eat, and the last to sleep since they were the clock of the camp. After all were called to breakfast, they were free to put their instruments aside and join the others in the mess line.

Charley held out his dish to the "scalped" corporal who scowled at him as he plopped a spoonful of beans on top of his dry bread and greasy bacon. Jamie, the bugler from the group, was just ahead of Charley. He turned and smiled, saying, "Got all your food? I'm starved. Let's find a place to eat."

They walked carefully, balancing plate in one hand and cup in the other. Hot coffee slopped over the side of the cup, burning Charley's hand. His stomach growled from the smell of coffee and bacon.

One of the soldiers called, "Here's a place, over here, boys."

Jamie and Charley sat with the group of men and began to eat. Charley took a gulp of coffee and promptly began to cough and sputter the steaming brew on the ground. The men burst out laughing.

"Better watch out, boy, that stuff will stunt your growth."

"Yer mama don't give ya nothin' like that at home."

Another burst of laughter from the men brought the threat of tears to Charley's eyes—whether from the thoughts of home or the burning coffee, he did not know.

"First taste of boiled rye, son?" asked one of the older men. "Better get used to it. We'll all be living on it before long, dunking our hardtack and warming our insides, once we've seen the elephant."

"It's just too hot," Charley mumbled. He gobbled down the beans and bread, then carefully drank coffee from the cup, trying to look as though he had been drinking coffee for many years. He did not think he would ever like its bitter taste or that it would ever taste "fine." Charley wanted to ask the old soldier with the beard about the elephants. Where were the elephants and were they really going to see one? But Charley had little time to think about that now. The boys had to finish breakfast, clean their mess kits, and prepare to sound sick call.

Even though there had not been time for wounds or sickness, sick call was a daily routine. Its drum rhythm seemed to say, "Come and get your quinine, come and get your quinine." The lone patient responding was a short broad man who hobbled, muttering all the way, "Ain't no cook. Ain't never meant to be no cook. I'm a pig farmer, that's what I am. Blasted iron pot fell on my foot. Ain't no cook!" Charley smiled as the wounded man disappeared into the tent.

"King, front and center," Sergeant O'Toole called. Charley hurried to the center of the encampment, wondering what he had done wrong. He could feel the eyes of the other boys on his back. He searched his mind for some reason that he had been singled out. "Yes, Sergeant?"

"I want you to escort the company guard to regimental head-quarters. Then return for drill."

As the four soldiers, rifles on shoulders, fell in behind Charley, O'Toole ordered, "Forward march."

The men stepped out—left, right, left, right. They moved forward smartly to the beat of Charley's drum. People stopped and looked. Others moved aside as he led the men out of camp. He filled with pride at the power his drum held.

Chapter Two

Lewinsville, Virginia —— September and October, 1861

"You, boy, come here! Now!"

Startled, Charley turned to see a tall officer with yellow hair to his shoulders.

"You, boy," he repeated.

"Me, sir?" Charley asked.

"Yes, you. Where are you going?"

"Back to camp, sir."

"Not until you shine my boots for me. Get in this tent, now!"

Charley was frightened by the size of the major who scowled and pointed toward his tent. "But, sir, I am not . . . "

Charley was cut off by the glowering major. "I said NOW! I've got to be at a meeting with General Hancock in fifteen minutes, and my boy's nowhere to be found. The blacking is on that shelf," he said pointing to a corner of the large permanent-looking tent.

Charley, who had followed the major into the tent, fumbled with his drum, setting it and the sticks on the wooden floor. Sergeant O'Toole had told him to return to camp immediately, yet this major had given him a direct order. He swallowed hard, trying to adjust his eyes to the darker interior of the tent. He picked up the polishing rag and boot black.

The major pulled off his boots, tossing them to Charley, and sat in front of his mirror. He looked at himself this way and that, running a comb through his hair and moustache and then flicking a piece of lint from his jacket. "I want to see my face shine in those boots, boy."

Charley spit on the boots and rubbed as hard as he could, trying to ignore the pain from his bruised arm. It seemed longer than ten minutes when the major took his gold watch from his pocket, snatched his boots from Charley, pulled them on, adjusted his saber, and strode out of the tent without a word.

Charley grabbed his drum and sticks and ran out into the bright sun. Back at camp, the regimental drum corps was marching in drill formation. Charley scrambled into place trying to pick up the cadence, aware of Sergeant O'Toole's side-long glance of disapproval and Frank Simpson's snicker.

The days passed in camp with what was becoming a well established routine. The clock of the regiment was what Sergeant O'Toole had called the lads of the drum corps and that is exactly what they were. As well as telling the soldiers when to awaken, eat, go to sick call, etc., the drum corps drilled and marched and marched and drilled, moving as one unit in precise time and rhythm across the parade ground.

The monotony of the drills tired, but also disciplined, the men and boys. By the end of the first week, Charley's painful bruises on his arm and neck had healed, but he still lay tense in his bunk each night, preparing himself for another attack from Frank Simpson. It never came, but he was aware of the animosity and jealousy that Frank felt toward him.

* * *

Frank Simpson watched Charley through eyes filled with envy. How could this little squint of a boy know all of the drum rolls so well, march so tall and straight, when other older boys, such as himself, were exhausted at the end of the day? Charley never showed fatigue. Oh, wasn't he the little pet of the company! From Sergeant O'Toole right down to the company cook, everyone knew Charley King and liked him. What is so special about him, Frank asked himself? He knew that he and Charley were the two best drummers vying for the position of drum major. He muttered aloud to himself, "Well, I don't know how yet, but somehow I'll make them all notice me and forget that little runt." Frank shifted his drum and banged the sticks harder, wishing it were the head of Charley King.

* * *

After three long weeks, Charley received his first letter from home. Day after day he had sounded mail call, but now he had nearly given up hope of hearing his own name shouted out. "King!" O'Toole said as he thrust a brown envelope toward Charley.

Instinctively, Charley looked for a private place to read his letter. He settled against the broad trunk of a tree along the creek bank and began to read:

West Chester, Pennsylvania
October, 1861

My Dear Son,

You are in our thoughts and prayers daily. The Reverend Weis reads out your name and all of the names of the brave young men from West Chester every Sunday at services. Papa and I are so proud. Give our regards to Captain Sweeney, and tell him that Papa has increased his business as Captain Sweeney promised. He has a government contract to make uniforms for our brave fighting men. Perhaps he will have to enlarge the premises and hire new workers. Your brothers and sisters are well and send their love. Grandpa Eb has taken a persistent cough. He speaks of you and Old Betsy. Charles, my son, stay close by Captain Sweeney's protection and do all he says. We await your safe return.

> *Your loving mother,*
> *Adaline King*

A surge of homesickness swept over Charley. He wanted more details of his brothers and sisters: Was Lewis taking over his old chores in the tailor shop—lighting the lamps, sweeping the floors? Did Ella like school? Was baby Anna walking? Just what had Captain Sweeney promised Papa and Mama? Was the government contract to make uniforms for the Union army the reason Papa had finally given him permission to enlist? He would take Mama's advice to stay near Captain Sweeney. But he had only seen him when the captain was too busy to notice. He sighed. Oh well, Mama doesn't understand how the army is run. Charley wished he could see his mama to ask these questions. How sick was Grandpa Eb? And what of Theo and Willie? Why did Mama not speak of them? He'd write home to ask just as soon as he got some time. Charley reached out to touch Old Betsy and felt closer to West Chester and Grandpa Eb.

Throughout the autumn the camp was transformed into winter quarters and a more permanent part of the defense of Washington. Although they had seen no action yet, occasional sniper fire from Confederate skirmishers was a reminder of the danger to the nation's capital. The tents gave way to log and mud huts, some lucky enough to be warmed by a small wood stove.

One day Charley and Frank Simpson found themselves in an uneasy truce, hauling buckets of mud from the creek bank to fill cracks between the logs of the huts to keep out the winter winds. Loud shouts and fast moving footsteps through the fallen leaves and twigs caught Charley's and Frank's attention. A lone man raced toward them followed at a distance by two soldiers with guns.

"Halt, or we'll shoot!" one yelled as he paused to raise his rifle to shoulder position.

The frantic man continued running, panting loudly, until he was stopped short by a log across the path and fell flat on his face. A shiny gold object flew from his hand in a sparkling arc glittering in the sun and landed at Frank's feet. Charley stared open-mouthed at the man sprawled in the path. His frightened eyes seemed to beg them for something, but the wind had been knocked from his lungs, and he couldn't speak. Charley reached down to retrieve what he saw was a gold watch, but Frank put his boot over the watch and pushed it into the mud, just as the two soldiers caught up with the fugitive.

"All right, where is it?" one of the soldiers said. "We know you stole the major's watch. Where is it?"

Charley opened his mouth to say something, but Frank gave him a terrific pound on the back, which made Charley cough and sputter.

"He's always choking," Frank said, explaining.

Charley remained silent. The fugitive soldier shot a look of gratitude toward the boys, as the two soldiers yanked him to his feet. They tied his hands behind him and, flanking him on each side, walked him back to camp.

"Why did you hide the watch?" Charley asked Frank when the men were out of earshot.

"You stupid runt!" Frank answered as he reached down and pulled the watch from the mud. "You heard the soldiers say it was a major's gold watch. I think the major sure would be grateful to get it back. Why, it might even be a watch his pa or grandpa gave him. Maybe he'll give a reward to two brave drummer boys who return his precious watch to him."

"Reward? But we didn't find it. The private dropped it when he fell."

"Then mind your own business, you namby pamby. I'll take care of this."

Charley shrugged and picked up his bucket of mud to head back to camp while Frank sat down on a log to clean the mud-caked watch.

Half an hour later Frank walked into camp without a sideways glance at the prisoner who was sitting on the ground, bucked and gagged. Charley could see Frank stop to ask a soldier something. The soldier motioned toward a group of officers outside one of the completed log huts. Charley recognized Captain Sweeney as well as the major with the long blonde hair, whose boots he had been ordered to shine. The major was angrily pacing back and forth, waving his arms, as he talked with the officers. Frank straightened his jacket and hat and approached the major, taking the watch from his pocket and extending it proudly. The major snatched the watch from Frank's hand and with one motion shoved Frank aside and strode toward the prisoner.

"Sergeant!" he thundered loud enough for all in the area to hear.

"Yes, sir," Sergeant O'Toole responded.

Pointing his finger at the prisoner, the major shouted, "I want this . . . this thief to receive full punishment. I want him divested of uniform, head shaven, and drummed out of this regiment. We have no room for cowardly thieves here!"

"Yes, sir!" Sergeant O'Toole responded again. He expected the major to leave the area, but when he stood there determined, waiting for his orders to be carried out, Sergeant O'Toole snapped out instructions.

"Simpson . . . you, King, Schmidt . . . get your drums and report back here directly."

The guards removed the gag from the prisoner's mouth and untied his wrists and ankles. His stiff legs were unable to support him, so he was dragged to a chair set in the middle of the parade ground. The toes of his boots left a trail in the dirt. While the major and other officers looked on, a sign which said "THIEF" in large black letters was hung around his neck. The prisoner sobbed quietly as the tall bald corporal, who also served as company cook, prepared to shave his head.

"Ha, Cook is happy doin' that. He wants everyone to look scalped like he is," Frank said to Charley with a laugh. But

Charley could not help feeling sorry for the hapless prisoner. The bile rose in Charley's throat. He watched the expression on the corporal's face with his protruding yellow horse-teeth covering his lower lip in concentration as he sharpened the blade on a leather strap and began to shave. Great clumps of brown hair fell to the ground.

Next, the drummers fell in behind the prisoner who was now standing, four soldiers guarding him front and back, bayonets at the ready.

"He sure ain't going to try to run for it. He can't hardly stand up," Hans said to Charley.

The drums rolled slowly as the stumbling, shaking prisoner was marched around the grounds for all to see. Then through the town to the outskirts, where he was left.

"Ain't nobody gonna help him with his head shaved like that," Hans said on the way back to camp.

"What will he do?" Charley asked.

"Make his way back to Pennsylvania best way he can," Hans replied.

"But he has no food," said Charley.

"Ain't nobody gonna give him any either, lest he can grow hair overnight," put in Frank. "Shaved head marks him a thief."

Charley wondered if the major's gold watch could ever have been worth the risk of all this misery and humiliation. And glancing at Frank, he wondered where the big reward was that Frank thought he would get from the major.

Chapter Three

Lewinsville, Virginia —— November and December, 1861

My Dear Mama and Papa,

I hope you are well. Please tell my brothers and sisters I am well and think of them often, as I do of you and home.

Charley sat with his back propped against the side of the log hut, writing his letter. The smoke from the stove inside burned his eyes, so he preferred to be outside where he could breathe fresh air.

I saw President Lincoln yesterday! He rode in an open carriage with his boy Tad at his side. The president sat so tall and straight. All the men felt proud to be reviewed by him. When he stepped down from the carriage, he looked like a giant. He shook hands with General Scott. The old general pulled himself up as tall as he could and saluted the president. Then his aides helped him into a carriage. The men say he resigned because he is too old and sick to command the army any longer. General McClellan now commands all our Federal troops. Mama and Papa, you would have thrilled

to see General McClellan mount his black horse and
salute as Mr. Lincoln rode away. We struck up a lively
tune. I think that old horse knew just how to prance to
the music. Tell Grandpa Eb that "Old Betsy" did him
proud.

We have not seen action yet, but have heard talk of
a skirmish at Ball's Bluff, Virginia. You may have read
in the newspaper that some of our boys' bodies floated
down the Potomac all the way to Washington!

Do not concern yourself, Mama, that I eat sufficient
food. Local peddlers come to camp almost daily with
fruit and homebaked pies and cakes, though not as tasty
as yours.

Please take care of yourselves all, and tell Grandpa
Eb I hope his cough is better.

Your loving son,
Charles King

Charley heard the clanging of pots and pans as the peddler
wagon pulled into camp. Putting his folded letter into his inside
pocket, he watched the wagon approach. Mr. Sinclair, who was
known to all in camp as having the best produce for sale, pulled
his mules to a stop. Jumping down from the wagon seat, he
handed the reins to his son and said, "You mind the mules and
wagon while I make my rounds."

Munching an apple, the boy looked down at Charley. "Hello,
want one?" he asked.

"Sure," Charley replied.

The boy reached behind the seat and in one motion, grabbed
an apple from the basket and threw it down to Charley.

Even though the boy looked kind of puny, he sure had a strong
throwing arm, Charley thought when the apple stung his hand.

"How old are you?" the boy asked, tossing his apple core to
the mules.

"Twelve," Charley answered, through a mouthful of apple.

"Me too. What's it like to be in the army?"

"All right I guess. Sometimes lonely, sometimes hard. Haven't seen any fighting yet. I can't wait to whip those Rebs. Mostly I play the drum and help out around camp."

"Sure sounds better than playing nursemaid to a couple of old mules," he said. "Wish I could be a drummer." He pulled his hat down tighter on his head.

"Why don't you ask your pa if you can join up to be a drummer?"

Before the boy could answer, Charley heard his name yelled, "King! We need you over here. Time to start the cook fires!"

Charley yelled his thanks for the apple as he ran toward the mess tent. Later while stacking wood beside the fire, Charley saw Mr. Sinclair return to the wagon. He tossed his empty sack in the back and took the reins. Charley watched as Sinclair reached over with his free hand and pulled the hat from his "son's" head in a friendly gesture. At the sight of a long blonde braid released from under the hat, Charley dropped an armful of kindling. He realized that the "boy" he had invited to join the drum corps was actually a girl!

Looking shyly in Charley's direction to see if he had noticed, she quickly retrieved her hat from the wagon seat and stuffed her long blonde hair under it. She slumped down into herself as if she were trying to become invisible. Charley, still confused, looked away pretending he had missed the whole episode. He didn't look up again until the wagon was out of sight, but he continued to wonder about the girl dressed as a boy.

It was three weeks later that Charley next saw Mr. Sinclair and his daughter. The weather had been cold, raining almost daily and turning the camp into a dismal sea of mud. The soldiers missed the occasional homemade pies, and they had finished their supply of apples and sweet potatoes a week ago. So when Mr. Sinclair's wagon rattled into camp one moderately dry afternoon, a crowd of soldiers greeted them. Charley stood on the outskirts and watched the girl climb down from the wagon seat. Mr. Sinclair was immediately caught up with the soldiers' requests, and the girl, shyly meeting Charley's eye and then looking away, slipped around the edge of the crowd to where Charley stood. She was still dressed as a boy in brown trousers, jacket, and hat pulled tightly on her head, but now Charley wondered how he had missed that slightly girlish walk and the few blonde curls that showed around the edge of the hat.

"Hello," she said.

Charley, shy now, looked at the ground. "Hello," he answered.

"What's your name?"

"Charley King. What's yours?"

"El Sinclair."

"El? What does that stand for?" Charley was beginning to enjoy the game now.

"Just El, that's all."

"Oh. Well, El, did your pa say you could join up?" Charley asked as the two moved over to where a group of fellows from the drum corps were standing.

"Who's this?" Frank Simpson interrupted. "Some little farm boy goin' to join up?" He gave El a shove which pushed her up against one of the other boys.

"Stop," Charley said. "Leave him be. This is El Sinclair. His pa is over there at the wagon. He wants to know what it's like to be a drummer."

"So you want to know about drumming," Frank said. "Well, you can't wear no stupid hat like this." Frank reached over to pull the hat from El's head. She grabbed the brim and held on tight.

"Leave off!" Charley said as he pushed Frank's arm away.

Still holding her hat brim, El swung her foot and gave Frank a hard kick on the shin. Frank howled in pain and grabbed his leg while Charley placed himself between the two. Frank, eyes blazing with anger, started swinging, and Charley was pushed into El, both falling to the ground. Diving in on top, Frank continued punching. El kicked furiously, and Charley struggled to protect her and push Frank off. The other fellows, seeing a good fight, circled around cheering and laughing. The three figures began to roll on the ground, first Frank on top, then El on top.

Suddenly the laughter and jeering stopped. Everything became quiet. El pulled herself off the top, grabbing her bare head with both hands. The circle of boys parted silently in wonder to let her pass through. Her yellow curls fell brightly around her mud-covered shoulders. "It's a girl," someone said as she ran to her father's wagon.

Frank sat open mouthed and motionless in the mud. "A girl? I fought a girl?" he said.

Charley pulled himself to his feet and scooped up the muddy, twisted object which had been El's hat. He followed her more slowly, giving the hat a futile brushing with his hand. She was resting her forehead against the side of the mule. Her eyes were closed, her shoulders shaking. Charley felt terrible. Here was the poor girl crying, and it was all his fault.

"I'm sorry, El," he said. "Here's your hat. Please don't cry."

She lifted her head and turned to him. To his surprise, she was not crying, but laughing. Her blue eyes danced with pleasure. "Oh, didn't we give him what for," she said and laughed again. "And don't you look a fine mess!"

Charley, looking down at himself, had to admit he did look a fine mess. He took the misshapen, wrinkled old hat and put it on her head. They both leaned together laughing and laughing until tears did come to their eyes, tears of laughter and friendship.

"What's your real name, El?" Charley asked when they had recovered from their laughter.

"Elspeth. Elspeth Sinclair." She formally extended a small hand in his direction. "Pleased to meet you, Charley King."

As Christmas approached, the encampment became more lively and almost a town in itself. Local peddlers came more and more often, selling goods for the soldiers to send home to their loved ones. The women of the town came to camp, looking for work washing the soldiers' uniforms and selling homemade canned goods from their own kitchens.

Charley and Elspeth were able to meet often and talk, sometimes walking along the creek, sometimes just standing beside the peddler's wagon as Elspeth helped her father.

"Hey, you little runt. How'd you get a girl, even though she wears overalls and fights like a boy?" teased Frank.

The question didn't really call for an answer, but Patrick spoke up. "I sure wish I could meet a girl, too. I get tired of looking at nothin' but your sour faces all the time."

"Aw, girls, who needs them?" said Frank. But Charley noticed that ever since Frank had fought with Elspeth, he had treated her with respect, though never actually had apologized to her.

One sunny cold afternoon they walked along the creek bank looking for firewood which was fast becoming scarce. Frank and Patrick were walking ahead of them, Patrick with a hand on his hip and the other hand extended before him in an exaggerated feminine walk. "Oh, Charles, you do look so handsome in your uniform," he said in a false, high pitched voice.

Frank, going along with the joke, swaggered and said, "Aw shucks, ma'am, I'm just an ordinary hero."

"Pay no attention to them, El," Charley said, tossing a clump of dirt in their direction.

"You sure are lucky to have brothers and sisters," Elspeth said, ignoring the teasing. "It must be wonderful having a houseful of people, especially during the holidays."

Charley nodded, realizing how much he would miss them this year. "Is it just you and your pa at home?" he asked.

"Yes. My mother died in childbirth two years ago, and my new baby brother died, too. I had to leave school to help my pa with the chores and do the cooking and housework. It gets mighty lonesome with no one to talk to." Elspeth paused. "Pa tries, but he's busy and not much of a talker. Sometimes at night we sit by the fire and read the Bible together."

"With five younger brothers and sisters at home, there was never any peace and quiet," Charley said. "Sometimes I wished that I were an only child, but now I know how you feel. I even miss little Willie's sticky fingers on my books and Anna's crying in the middle of the night."

Christmas Eve was clear and cold. The cook fires blazed all day as the camp cooks worked hard to make special food for the holiday. Charley was excited to receive a large parcel from home: cookies from Mama, and warm socks and a muffler that she knit for him; from little Theo, a drawing that he supposed was himself in a uniform of blue and a big hat with a red plume, sitting atop of something that resembled a horse. Charley smiled at the thought of his little brother concentrating hard, his tongue sticking out, as he tried his best to become an artist.

Each member of the family had added something to the parcel. Grandpa Eb had sent his best whittling knife. "His eyes are not good enough to carve any longer, Charles, so he wants you to have this." Charley rubbed his eyes as he read the note from home. Best of all, at the very bottom of the package, he found a new, beautiful blue uniform made in his father's tailor shop just for him! As he tried on the warm wool tunic, he pictured the workshop and his father's loving hands pinning and cutting, deftly and surely. He suddenly longed for the familiar warmth of the workshop and home.

*   *   *

Frank watched from his bunk in the corner of the hut as Charley admired gift after gift. That runt has everything, he thought, a sweetheart, letters from home, a home to go home to, for that matter. And the trouble was, he was likable! He made friends with everyone! After that first night when he had bullied Charley, Frank knew he'd never do anything that obvious again. No one would go along with him. And the little squint had never even told on him. He had to give him that much. Charley was not a cry baby. But how would the little runt hold up in battle?

Probably run home to Mama. Frank knew he himself would hold up in battle. After all, he'd had to fight all his life.

*   *   *

The boys compared gifts of cookies and sweets as Jamie opened a parcel and began to pull a blue and white muffler from the wrapping.

"Hey, look what my girl at home made for me!" he shouted. The boys gathered around him laughing while Jamie pulled yards and yards of knitted material from the package.

"She sure thinks you've grown some," Hans laughed.

"Yeah, is that supposed to be a muffler or a tent?" Charley joked.

"Frank, come look at this," said Patrick.

Frank remained on his bunk in the dark shadows of the hut. He did not share the cookies or the fun of the other boys, but instead turned his back to them and faced the wall. "Sure am glad I don't have any stupid girl knitting me any nine foot muffler," he growled.

The boys fell into an awkward silence, for the first time realizing that Frank had received nothing from home. Finally Patrick said, "Well, I have work to do. See you later." He put on his new gloves and left the hut. The others followed Patrick's lead till Charley was left alone with the silent disgruntled figure in the corner of the hut. After he put more wood on the fire in the small stove, Charley held out the tin of ginger cookies his mama had sent him. "Come on, Frank, it's Christmas time. Have a cookie."

Frank shrugged without turning. "Christmas don't mean anything to me. Just another day, that's all. Leave me be."

Charley, not knowing what else to say, put on his new uniform in honor of the holiday, and, leaving Frank to his misery, went outside to wait for Elspeth's and Mr. Sinclair's expected visit. He wanted to share his gifts from home with El. He knew she would enjoy the drawing from Theo, and he hoped she would admire his new knife from Grandpa Eb. The company had been relieved of afternoon drill, so Charley with free time on his hands wandered the camp. He stopped to visit with various soldiers who were sitting around fires playing the ever popular card games.

When the wagon pulled into camp, jingling with Christmas bells on the mules' harnesses, Charley forgot all about showing El his new knife. Sitting on the wagon seat next to Mr. Sinclair was the most beautiful girl he had ever seen! Gone were the usual trousers and floppy hat. Instead, her small face was framed by a green velvet bonnet, and her gold curls, released from their plait, fell softly over her shoulders and her dark green cloak. Her hands were concealed in a green velvet muff. As the wagon came to a halt, she turned her face in Charley's direction and smiled at him. It was as if the sun had just come out. Charley stared.

Mr. Sinclair swung down from the wagon and walked around to his daughter's side. "May I help you, miss?" he said, reaching his arms up to assist Elspeth from the wagon.

"Oh, Papa," El laughed as she leaned forward so her father could swing her to the ground.

Charley had not moved. Elspeth walked toward him. "Happy Christmas," she said, smiling again at Charley.

At last he found his voice. "Happy Christmas to you too, El. You look so . . . so different."

"Do you like it?" she asked, turning so that Charley could enjoy the full benefit of her new outfit. "Papa gave me this for Christmas."

As the others gathered around the wagon to see what they could buy, shouts and whistles were directed toward Elspeth. "Hey, where's your overalls?" "Want to fight now?" The remarks were followed by loud laughter until Mr. Sinclair turned to the soldiers with a scowl.

Elspeth blushed from the sudden attention directed at her, and Charley pulled her away from the crowd. "You look very pretty. I . . . I just never saw you in a dress before," he said.

"You look very grand, too," Elspeth said, touching the fine wool of his new uniform.

"My father made it for me in his tailor shop," Charley said proudly. "I received the parcel today."

"Oh, I have something for you," said Elspeth, suddenly remembering. She turned and, forgetting her long skirts, began to run toward the wagon, tripping and stumbling. Quickly recovering her balance, she hiked up the troublesome skirt and petticoat to her knees and ran to where Mr. Sinclair was standing. She spoke to him, and he handed her a round packet wrapped in brown paper. Turning, she demurely walked back to Charley and said, "For you, Charley King. I made it myself."

"Thank you, El," Charley said as he opened the paper to reveal a sweet currant cake still warm from the oven. "This looks delicious! Just like what my mother bakes for Christmas." Realizing he had nothing to give in exchange, Charley pushed his hand into the pocket of his trousers and felt Grandpa Eb's knife. As his fingers closed around the surface of the leather sheath, he thought for a fleeting moment of giving it to El. He could almost feel the imprint of Eb's strong fingers beneath his own, and he knew he could not be parted from this symbol of his grandpa's love. "Wait right here. Don't move," he said to El, placing his hand on her shoulder.

Charley ran as fast as he could around men who were piling high wood pyramids for the Christmas Eve bonfires. He arrived out of breath at the door of the hut. As he entered, he saw Frank standing by the stove, stroking the new red muffler. His face looked sad and lonely.

Frank dropped the muffler on the bunk. "Just looking," he said. "I didn't mean no harm."

"That's all right, Frank," said Charley. He picked up the muffler. "It's nice, isn't it? Would be warm on a cold night, but I reckon I couldn't wear it outside with my uniform. I'm going to give it to Elspeth for Christmas."

Frank shrugged. "Looks more like a girl anyway."

"Yes, that's what I thought," said Charley. Frank's face was now expressionless, but Charley knew he had not mistaken the pain and loneliness he had seen there a few moments before.

By the time Charley had retraced his steps to where he had left El, she was gone. He ran toward the main road of the camp in time to see Elspeth perched on the wagon seat next to her father, anxiously watching for Charley. He reached the wagon out of breath.

"Can't stop for long. We've got a lot of ground to cover before dark," Mr. Sinclair said impatiently as he halted the mules.

Charley nodded and handed the red muffler up to Elspeth. "Happy Christmas, El. My mother made it. Happy Christmas, Mr. Sinclair."

Elspeth smiled in delight as she wrapped the scarlet muffler around her neck over the dark green of her cloak, looking like Christmas itself. The wagon lurched forward. Charley stood and watched as they drove out of sight, El waving to him all the way.

As midnight approached, the camp was ablaze with the Christmas bonfires. The sparks shot high into the winter night sky as the men stood or sat near enough to be warmed by the flames. The shadows and light fell across the faces of all, from the young boys of the drum corps to the older men with gray beards. They talked of home and family and wondered aloud if the Christmas of 1861 would be their last.

One of the old timers, Jacob Adams, the bearded man who had talked to Charley the first day about seeing an elephant, brought out his fiddle. He played familiar melody after melody, both cheery and mournful. Some of the men joined in with harmonicas, and when Patrick brought out his fife, Sergeant O'Toole was coaxed into dancing an Irish jig. He seemed to grow wings on his feet. O'Toole, with his broad frame, leapt and stamped the ground in perfect rhythm. His shadow, now looming large, now becoming small, fell across the amazed boys of the drum corps. Their sergeant twirled and stamped in time with the lilting, mystical music of the fife and fiddle in a timeless dance.

At midnight the camps burst into celebration as men shot guns into the sky, and buglers and drummers heralded the arrival of

Christmas Day. After much cheering, handshaking, and back slapping, the camp grew more silent. Jacob Adams in his baritone began to sing "Silent night, holy night." The men and boys joined in, "All is calm, all is bright . . . " Charley could hear another camp singing a few bars behind, almost like a round. Camp after camp took up the song until the whole night was filled with the reverent sound of men's voices. Vibrating the very ground beneath their feet, the voices rose with the sparks from the fires into the night air, reverberating across the fields and woods into the town so that people came out of their houses to listen. "Sleep in heavenly peace, Sleep in heavenly peace."

When the last notes faded, it truly became a silent night. Each man sat with his own thoughts. Charley was aware of a muffled sob coming from the shadows behind him. In the dim light he saw Frank Simpson, huddled alone, wipe his hand across his eyes.

Chapter Four

Lewinsville, Virginia —— February, 1862

By early February of 1862, Charley was depressed. A deep freeze, as he was used to in Pennsylvania, had not settled in. Instead, the climate was cold, wet, miserable—freezing and thawing with slush and raw sewage from the encampments running or standing in fields and trenches everywhere. The stench permeated his bed linens, his clothing, and even the cold air outside. Diseases such as typhoid, cholera, and measles had placed the camp under quarantine.

Charley had a constant cold and cough, but somehow he had withstood the more serious epidemics. Instead of lying on his cot burning with fever as so many others, he now helped care for the sick. He had not seen Elspeth since Christmas Eve because no one was allowed to enter or leave the camp. Supplies were left outside the gates for soldiers to carry in. He wished he could walk along the creek, breathe fresh air, and talk of ordinary things with El as they had done in the autumn. He wondered what she would think of his "grand" uniform now after he had helped carry many sick or dying soldiers to the hospital tent and emptied countless slop jars.

Bone weary at the end of the day, Charley lit a candle and took out the letter from home which he had not had time to read earlier.

West Chester, Pennsylvania
February, 1862

My dear son Charles,

    It is with a heavy heart that I write to you this sad news. Your grandfather, my father, Ebenezer Maitland Holt died last Thursday, the sixth of February, at five in the evening. He died in his sleep of pneumonia, "the old man's friend," as Dr. Morgan calls it. He spoke of you near the end. You were often in his thoughts, Charles. We shall miss him, but God in his wisdom has taken him from us. Pray for us all, Charles, as we pray for you.

Your loving mother,
Adeline King

Charley read the letter, then read it again. He could not believe that Grandpa Eb had died. This war had changed his life, but he had always expected home to stay the same. Now home could never be the same again without Grandpa Eb! So much death! Charley thought of his friend Jamie, who had died just the other day of measles. He had helped to carry Jamie to the hospital tent, so full of fever that he was moaning and talking gibberish. Now he was dead, and even the tough Frank Simpson was sick. Maybe he, too, would die.

"Is this supposed to be war?" Charley thought. "We haven't seen a battle yet, but still men are dying." He sat on his bunk in the deserted hut and cried, not only for Grandpa Eb, but for Jamie and all the others who sicken and die far from home and family. "I hope it doesn't happen to me," he whispered into the darkness.

Signs of spring helped to lift some of the depression which lay over the camps. A haze of yellow-green buds and their promise of first leaves appeared on the trees. General McClellan, now recovered from a bout with typhoid fever, held massive reviews of the troops to raise the morale. Rumors had spread that President Lincoln himself was impatient with General McClellan's hesitancy to move against the enemy at Manassas. But the splendor of the grand reviews, with McClellan riding the lines and inspecting the troops while President Lincoln looked on, helped to restore the general's popularity.

Company F of the Pennsylvania 49th Volunteers was ordered to participate in a huge review at Bailey's Crossroads. Frank Simpson appeared gaunt and pale, still weak from his sickness and without vigor for the march. Charley, on the other hand, was full of confidence and in full uniform which he had aired and brushed clean. Once again Charley felt the power of his drum as he marched, beating perfect time for the men to follow. Assorted carriages and wagons surrounded the parade ground as townspeople and wealthy landowners watched the troops pass in review. It had been a nasty winter and all were happy to share this diversion. Some had picnic lunches and had settled in for a long day of enjoyment.

As they approached the grandstand where he knew President and Mrs. Lincoln were seated and "Little Mac" was inspecting the lines, Charley pulled himself as straight as he could and lifted his knees high with each step. From the corner of his eye, Charley saw a figure in a calico dress with gold hair glistening in the sun push her way to the front of the crowd. He recognized Elspeth Sinclair, and his heart leapt inside him. So filled with pride was he that as he came abreast of where Elspeth was standing and he was sure her eyes were on him, he tossed his drum stick into the air and caught it without missing a beat. Thinking he could not go wrong, he tossed it again even higher. But this time it did not land conveniently in his hand. Instead it hit his hat and glanced off to the ground on the right. Horrified, Charley snatched it up as quickly as possible before the mass of troops following behind trampled him. Why had he done such a thing! O'Toole would kill him! He glanced sideways to see if his disastrous mistake had been noticed. "Little Mac" was looking at the approaching troops, and President Lincoln was busy, whispering behind his hand to Mrs. Lincoln. So maybe no one had noticed, except El, and he knew she had seen it.

Charley continued marching to the end of the line, feeling his face blazing red with embarrassment, and careful to keep exact rhythm with no more fancy movements. When Company F of the Pennsylvania 49th had completed their part of the review, they assembled to await further orders. Charley stood off to the side, not wanting to talk with anyone.

Sergeant O'Toole approached the group, eyes blazing, his red moustache quivering. "King! Front and center!" Charley was conscious of a snicker from Frank Simpson as he turned to face the sergeant.

"What in blue blazes do ya think ya were doing out there? Showin' off at precisely the wrong moment! That little bit of vanity could have jeopardized the whole company's performance before Mr. Lincoln himself!"

Charley's humiliation increased as O'Toole's voice grew louder with each word. He could feel the eyes of the others burning into his back. He wanted to disappear into a big black hole and not come out again. "I'm sorry, Sergeant, I . . ."

"Quiet! And stand at attention!" O'Toole bellowed. At that moment a messenger approached and handed the sergeant an envelope. O'Toole read the note, and the color drained from his face.

"Well, it looks as though your little display was noticed in high places, King. You're wanted at General McClellan's reception tent immediately."

Charley felt his knees grow weak. General McClellan . . . what could that mean? Would he be drummed out in disgrace as the thief was? Head shaven and alone? Whatever happened, it could be no worse than the wrath of O'Toole.

Charley followed the sergeant toward the large tent which had been set up for the dignitaries. After they were out of sight of the others, Sergeant O'Toole placed a hand on Charley's shoulder. "Now listen to me, laddie, this is important. Speak only when spoken to. Respond with yes, sir, no, sir. If ladies speak to you, it's yes, ma'am, no, ma'am. And remember, you represent Company F of the Pennsylvania 49th Volunteers in all you say and do. So look sharp, keep your wits about ya. And we'll get through this."

"Sergeant O'Toole and drummer King reporting as ordered, sir," O'Toole saluted the young captain at the entrance of the reception tent.

"Very good, Sergeant. You wait over there." The captain gestured in the direction of the outskirts of the large tent. "King, follow me."

Charley turned frightened eyes toward O'Toole, who nodded his head slightly as if to say, "Just remember what I told you and you'll be all right." Charley swallowed hard and followed the ramrod-straight blue tunic of the captain through a crowd of men and women; some men in uniform, some not, all too busy to notice a boy wide-eyed and frightened.

The captain stopped in front of a group of ladies. He bent to speak to a small woman who seemed to be the center of the group. The woman turned to face Charley. She was not much taller than he, with chestnut brown hair and vivid blue eyes in a weary and somber face.

"Mrs. Lincoln, may I present drummer Charles King of the Pennsylvania 49th Volunteers."

"Ah . . .," Mrs. Lincoln gave a nod of recognition and then turned with a quick thank you and dismissal to the captain. "Charles King," she repeated. "I am very pleased to meet you, young man."

Charley's mouth was dry from nervousness, but he licked his lips and managed to say with a slight bow of his head, "Yes, ma'am. Pleased to meet you, ma'am."

"You're very young to be such an impressive drummer of our great army. How old are you?"

"I'm twelve, ma'am." His voice seemed to croak when he spoke.

"And where did you gain your skill? Surely you have not acquired such talent entirely from your months in training during the defense of Washington."

"No, ma'am. My grandfather taught me, ma'am. He was a drummer in the war of 1812." Charley was finding his voice a little more easily now. Looking at the kindly expression of Mary Todd Lincoln, he felt a sense of relief.

"Mr. Lincoln and I so enjoyed the review, most especially your extraordinary performance."

"Yes, ma'am. I mean thank you, ma'am. I'm sorry I . . ."

"Now, come over here with me. There's someone I'd like you to meet."

President Lincoln was busy talking with General McClellan and a group of officers. He stood head and shoulders above the men surrounding him. His laughter boomed louder than that of his companions. Charley saw when the president turned in response to Mrs. Lincoln's request, that although he laughed, his eyes, deeply set in the lined face, were sad.

"Mr. Lincoln, I would like you to meet drummer Charles King, who so impressed us during the review."

"Well, well." The president placed a hand on the boy's shoulder. Charley had to tilt his head back in order to see the face of the tall man before him. At the president's side stood General McClellan, who reached just below Lincoln's shoulder. Charley could see why the men called the general "Little Mac." He looked so much taller astride his grand black horse.

McClellan cast a cold look in Charley's direction, as though he were annoyed at the interruption of this bothersome little woman and her interest in this insignificant drummer. Charley was startled by the look he saw in the eyes of the general, but as quickly as it came, it vanished and was replaced by a cordial expression. Excusing himself, Little Mac directed his attention toward a group of congressmen and their ladies, who were not far away.

Lincoln looked down at Charley. "Your marching is grand." Then, lowering his head even further, he whispered, "But your baton tossing requires a bit more practice."

Charley felt the warmth creeping up his neck, and he knew his face was turning crimson.

"Now, Father," Mrs. Lincoln said as she placed her small hand on the president's arm. A look of sadness came over her face. She spoke softly to her husband. "He has blue eyes, like our Willy's."

Lincoln placed a protective arm around the small woman who suddenly looked very lonely. He motioned to the captain. "Please see that this young soldier has refreshment," he said and then led Mrs. Lincoln away.

As Charley approached the refreshment table, his mouth was as dry as cotton. He settled himself on a small chair with a large lemonade and some delicious cake that tasted unlike anything he had ever eaten. After gulping down lemonade to quench his thirst, he took more time to enjoy the cake. As he licked the final crumbs from his fingers, he glimpsed Sergeant O'Toole standing with his hands behind his back and craning his neck to see into the tent. Charley knew that the sergeant was looking for him. Picking up another piece of cake, Charley slipped out of the tent unnoticed.

"The captain said we are free to leave," said Charley. "Would you like a piece of cake, Sergeant?"

Sergeant O'Toole had snapped to attention as soon as he heard Charley's voice, but visibly relaxed when he saw Charley was alone. Ignoring the cake, O'Toole placed a strong hand at the base of Charley's neck and propelled him rapidly away from the area of the reception tent. Charley, taking two steps to O'Toole's one, tried to look up at the sergeant's face but the steady hand at his neck held him firmly. Out of sight of the tent, O'Toole stopped and finally released his hold on Charley.

"Have some cake, Sergeant. Very good cake it is, Sergeant," he said in a high pitched mimic. "Oh, butter wouldn't melt in your mouth. What did he say ta ya, boy-O?"

"Do you mean Mr. Lincoln, Sergeant?"

"Yes, yes, laddie, our commander in chief, the president of these United States, Abraham Lincoln! Who da ya think I mean?"

Charley saw the color flare in Sergeant O'Toole's cheeks. "Well, Sergeant, he said my marching was grand, but my baton tossing requires a bit more practice."

O'Toole threw his head back in booming laughter. As the two approached Company F, O'Toole was still chuckling and polishing off the remains of "Mrs. Lincoln's cake."

*   *   *

Frank Simpson had been slumped against a wagon wheel alongside Patrick as the men awaited orders to return to camp. When he heard O'Toole's laughter and saw Charley's happy face, his heart sank. "Look at that cocky little bantam rooster," Frank said to Patrick. "Thinks he's cock of the walk."

"I sure thought he was in for it this time, but it looks like everything is all right now," Patrick replied.

As the boys of the corps gathered around Charley, Frank sullenly hung off to the side. He shoved his hands into his pockets and looked at the ground. He was so tired, and his back ached. The marching for the grand review had taken every ounce of energy he had, and now all he wanted to do was get back to camp and collapse on his bunk. But here was this "little King," full of energy, the center of attention, just back from talking to the president himself. Wouldn't be surprised if Little Mac promoted him to colonel before he even sees his first battle, Frank thought sarcastically. Why, he didn't even get sick this winter like most of us.

*   *   *

Chapter Five

Advance on Manassas —— March, 1862

At dawn the morning of March 10 the rain fell in torrents. Charley had already been awake for hours, in fact he had barely slept two hours during the night.

"I can't believe we're finally doing something after all these months of drilling and waiting, waiting and drilling," said Patrick ecstatically. "Once we get to Manassas we'll show Johnston and his Rebs a thing or two."

"Yeah, we'll show them," Charley had added, playing a quick little roll on his drum for emphasis.

That had been last evening when they first received the order. Now after a night of working in shifts to pack up medical supplies and countless litters and dismantling the mess tent, they were less enthusiastic.

"Don't think we're gonna be doing much fighting through all this rain. Why, you can't see more than three feet in front," Patrick said as the boys packed up the supplies.

"Bullets and cannon fire don't need to see you to hit you," Frank replied.

They were lucky to grab a breakfast of strong, scalding coffee and hardtack before the fires were doused. Bugles and drum rolls sounded throughout the camp, muted by the pounding rain which turned the walks and roads into mud. Charley had stood beating his drum, hat drawn over his forehead, cape collar turned up at the back of his neck. There was little protection from the persistent rain. The log huts stood open to the sky now that the canvas tent roofs had been dismantled and packed away. Wrapping his drum in oilskin to protect it from the effect of the wetness, Charley tried to find a quiet place to rest for a moment. But apparently no quiet place existed anywhere in the camp this day.

While standing under a tree which offered scant protection, he saw the figure of Elspeth Sinclair. For a moment, Charley felt as if the clouds had lifted. He watched her stepping carefully, peeking out from under her hooded cape, searching the faces around her. She had not seen him yet. He simply stood watching the small figure through the rain. Then, raising his arm, he shouted above the noise, "El, over here!"

She heard his voice and stopped, looking around to locate the sound. Then she saw him and smiled the brightest smile he had ever seen. Without care for puddles or obstacles, she ran toward him, hood fallen back and bright hair bouncing in the rain.

"Oh, I'm so glad I got here in time to see you before you leave," Elspeth said.

"Here, you're getting soaked," Charley said as he pulled El's hood back up over her head. His hand lingered longer than necessary against the moist curls.

They huddled back further, closer to the tree, trying to get some protection from the relentless rain.

"I was afraid I wouldn't see you again, El. I made something for you." Fumbling beneath cape and tunic, he took out a tiny carving and handed it to her.

"Why, it's my old mule Nelson! How did you manage it?"

"I've been working on it in my spare time since Christmas with Grandpa Eb's whittling knife. Hope you like it."

"Oh, I do. It's beautiful! Thank you, Charley. I have a keepsake for you, too." She produced a small drawstring leather pouch.

Charley held it close and looked inside. Shining brightly against the dark material was a ringlet of El's hair, tied with a blue ribbon. He caught his breath when he saw it. "Oh, El, thank you."

"It's a forget-me-not pouch so that you can remember me."

"I will, El. I could never forget you!"

"Simpson, King, Lynch! Report here on the double!" O'Toole's booming voice interrupted.

"I have to go, El."

"Write to me, Charley King. My address is in the pouch," she said. Then quickly she kissed him, turned, and ran through the crowded camp. He stood stunned, his hand on his face where she had kissed him. Elspeth turned once, half lifted her hand in a parting gesture, then was gone.

"King!" Sergeant O'Toole growled, "Now . . . move!"

Charley's attention was reluctantly drawn back to O'Toole. "Yes, Sergeant," he answered, and ran over to join the members of the drum corps. Elspeth hadn't actually said good-by and neither had he, he thought. He was sure they would see each other again. His eyes searched the grounds for one last glimpse of her, but she had disappeared.

"I see your tomboy sweetheart came to see you off," Frank said.

Charley clenched his fists, instantly ready to defend any slight to Elspeth, and turned to face Frank. But the look on Frank's face was more envious than menacing, and Charley let the remark pass. Involuntarily his hand went again to his cheek where Elspeth had kissed him and then to his pocket where he had placed the forget-me-not pouch.

Patrick said, "It looks like the whole town has turned out to see us off. Do you think they're sad or happy to see us go?"

Indeed, the whole town did seem to be out in spite of the early hour and the drenching rain! As the army moved southward toward

Manassas, the crowds of well-wishers around Washington, D.C. which had cheered them on, gave way to deserted streets and shuttered houses. Occasionally a window curtain would separate slowly to reveal a still form observing, only to close again quickly as the troops marched by. Charley beat his drum and pounded through the wet streets.

As evening approached, the heavy rain diminished to a fine mist. The company bivouacked in an open field near the town of Fairfax Court House. Charley and Frank were sent by the cook to retrieve some wood for the fire.

"I don't care if it's tree or fence, but don't come back empty-handed," he said.

Trudging toward the town, Frank was sullen as usual, and Charley wondered where they could get dry wood. Frank spotted some firewood stacked in an open shed in the yard of a small house.

"There's our wood," he said to Charley. "Come on!" Frank was over the fence and collecting the wood in a sack before Charley could think of what to do. "Come on, King. I need your help," Frank shouted, annoyed at Charley's reluctance.

"Sure looks like these folks don't have much," Charley said.

"Oh, come on! Orders is orders."

As Charley was just about to climb the fence, he saw the door of the house open just a crack and the shiny barrel of a gun stick out. "Frank, look out!" he shouted as he hurled himself over the fence, landing on top of Frank and the sack of wood.

A woman stepped out on the porch, a small child clinging to her skirt. Leveling the gun at the two on the ground, she said, "You Yankees leave me and my younguns alone. That's my wood, and it ain't intended to warm no Yankee backsides. Now git!"

"Let's get out a' here!" Frank shouted. The two vaulted back over the fence and ran for cover. Slipping and sliding on the wet cobbled streets, they turned a corner and fell back against the side of a barn.

"Do you think she really would shoot us?" Charley said as he tried to catch his breath.

"She's a Reb, ain't she?"

For the first time Charley realized that he was an enemy. How many of these quiet looking houses held Rebels with guns, peering through window or doors, watching them right this minute? Charley shivered at the thought.

As the two reached the front of the barn, walking more cautiously now and still searching for wood, they were startled by the sudden appearance of a frantic looking boy of about nine. His shirt sleeves were rolled up and his forearms were splattered with blood. The three stood in silent surprise, staring at each other. A deep bellow from within the darkness of the barn broke the silence.

"Please help me!" he said to the two young soldiers. "Please, Bessie's calving, and there's just Grandma. And she can't do no helping. Hurry, please!"

Frank and Charley looked at each other. Frank shrugged, and they followed the boy inside the barn. In the dim light of a stall they saw a cow standing, a pool of blood beneath her, a tail and leg protruding from her hind quarters.

"See? She's calving, but it won't come out. I tried!" the boy said, his eyes filling with tears. "She's all Grandma and me have left. If she dies . . ." His voice trailed off. He sank to the floor on his knees in exhausted defeat.

"Here, get up! Bring that lantern over here," Frank said to the boy, taking charge of the situation. Then removing his tunic and shirt, Frank placed them on a pile of clean straw. "King, get me that rope hanging over yonder. You," he said to the boy, "stand by her head, talk to her. Make sure she don't lie down. Hurry with that rope, and take off that tunic," he said to Charley.

Frank, struggling, guided the rope inside the cow in order to wrap it around the upper hind legs of the calf. "Here now, King, get behind me. And when I say 'pull,' lean hard into it." Frank, his arms inside the cow, guided the calf forward as he shouted to Charley, "Pull! Now stop! Pull! Here she comes. One more. Pull!"

And with a great whoosh and a deep moan from Bessie, the calf slid out into Frank's arms. With the sudden release of tension in the rope, Charley fell backwards onto the floor of the stall and stayed there in wonder as he watched Frank gently lay the calf on clean straw at its mother's feet. Immediately Bessie turned to lick and clean her baby. The calf bleated pitifully at first and then more strongly as it struggled awkwardly to its feet and crowded closer to the warmth of its mother. It searched blindly and instinctively for the udder, and finally succeeding, sucked noisily.

Charley and Frank burst out laughing as the young boy danced around shouting, "You did it, Bessie, you did it!"

"What do you mean Bessie did it? We did it! Bessie was not much help at all," Frank said as he reached a hand down to Charley to help him up.

"You surely did do it, and I thank you," a voice said from the doorway of the barn.

"Grandma, Grandma, look at our new calf! Ain't she grand? She's got the same black tail and black ring around the eyes as Bessie!"

"Yes, yes, she's grand enough, Horace." The old woman entered the barn. Walking slowly she placed a basin of steaming water and some towels on a bench near the door. "Here's some water and lye soap to clean yourselves up. When you finish, come into the house for some vittles by way of thanks."

Frank spoke up. "Thank you, ma'am, but we need to report back to our company. We just came out to get us some wood for cooking. We've been gone too long already."

"Humph. Your company is it? Town is packed with Yankees I expect. Well, no matter. I've seen fights come and go. When all's said and done, folks are just folks and need to get along with each other. There's good and bad on both sides." Then, turning to her grandson, "Horace, you go now to the woodpile and fill that sack with wood for these two good Samaritan Yanks."

"Thank you, ma'am." Charley found his voice, and the old woman nodded as she walked slowly out of the barn.

Charley and Frank took turns plunging their arms into the warm water and lathering the soap up to their elbows. "Sure would feel good to step into a whole tub of this hot water, wouldn't it?" said Charley, trying to make conversation with the now silent Frank.

"I ain't never had the luxury of soaking in a whole tub of water," Frank muttered. "Ain't never had no home that cared if I cleaned up or not, except when the inspectors from the Orphan's Society came around. Then we got cleaned up good and proper. Just got to borrow the new shoes and clothes. They got put away as soon as the inspectors left."

Charley straightened up and looked at Frank with sympathy. "Is that where you learned to birth a cow?" he asked.

"I just know, that's all. All right?" Frank said.

*　　*　　*

Birthin' a cow had come right back to him, hadn't it, Frank thought. Yeah, that and all the other memories that went along with it. As he soaped his arms, Frank could see in his mind the farm in the hills of Pennsylvania where he and Meg had been "let out" by the orphan asylum as workers. Oh, he knew about cows all right. He and Meg had slept in the barn with all the cows. At least he had been able to steal some milk for Meg. Old man Kleinmetz had beaten him every time he didn't know how to do something like mend a fence or plow a field. But how was he to know without bein' shown first? And then there was the way Kleinmetz had looked at Meg. He hadn't liked that either. No, they had been better off back at the orphanage than stayin' on that farm. But Meg. . . . No, he wouldn't let himself think about Meg now.

*   *   *

"Come on, get a move on. Or mother hen O'Toole will be all over us like fleas on a dog," Frank said to Charley.

They rubbed their arms dry with the rough towels and were buttoning their tunics when Horace returned, dragging two heavy burlap sacks of firewood. Thanking him, they each shouldered a sack and hurried out into the fresh damp air, breathing deeply after the pungent animal smells of the barn. It was dusk as they hurried back to camp on the outskirts of town.

"Took yuz long enough," the cook grumbled as they dumped the sacks beside an already burning campfire. "I had to send the other boys out, and they came back with fence rails. Where'd yuz get this dry wood? Never mind, I won't ask," he grunted. "There's chicken stew over yonder. Won't say where we got that neither. But yuz two eat up or there won't be none left."

Trying to warm themselves against the evening chill, Charley and Frank squatted next to the fire to eat their stew. Charley threw half of his tin mug of coffee into the fire. As it sputtered on the flames, he said, "I never have learned to like that stuff."

"Shhh, quiet," Hans said. "Listen."

The others around the fire raised their heads and listened to the steadily increasing roar of a great number of men's voices.

"Must be a fight," Frank said. "Sounds like a crowd yelling."

"That's no small fight," Jacob Adams said, standing, brushing crumbs from his beard. "Too big for that. More a riot, likely."

The whole company, some picking up their guns uncertainly, followed the noise into town. Charley, Frank, Hans, and Patrick were swept along with them, all the way to the square where the old Fairfax Courthouse stood. The entire Union army seemed to be there, gone raving mad! Men were breaking the windows, storming through the doors!

Charley watched one soldier, who was very tall and broad, standing in the open rectangle of the courthouse door. He wrenched the door from its hinges. Holding it above his head, both arms raised as high as possible, he hurled it down the court-house steps into the square. Crashing to the ground, the heavy door split as men leapt out of the way, laughing and cheering. The tall soldier swaggered down the steps, took a jug from a companion, raised it to his shoulder, threw his head back, and took a long drink. Turning the jug over to make sure he had emptied it, he smashed it to the ground. A surge of blue coats streamed up the littered steps and was swallowed by the gaping opening that had been a door.

More and more men seemed to be drawn into this strange violence. Charley and Patrick watched in amazement as Frank and Hans eagerly joined in the wanton destruction. Papers, ledgers, and valuable old books were torn from their files and shelves, ripped apart, and strewn on the floors. As bookcases were lifted and thrown through the windows to the cobbled stones below, the sound of glass shattering mingled with the roar of the crowd.

Captain Sweeney and Sergeant O'Toole spoke nearby, but Charley could not hear their words above the uproar. In desperation, Captain Sweeney raised his pistol straight up and shot twice into the air. A few soldiers nearby took only momentary notice. Looking at O'Toole, the captain raised his arms in a helpless gesture.

Charley wondered what the people of the town were thinking and where they were hiding. He thought of the young Horace, Bessie and her new calf, and especially of the fine old woman who had said, "There's good and bad on both sides." Tonight he could see only bad.

Charley and Patrick turned and walked wordlessly back to camp. The shouts faded into the background. Charley crawled into his tent, exhausted, and fell asleep.

"Forward March!" The command came early the next morning. Charley and the other drummer boys beat out a steady marching rhythm as the regiment moved down the road through the center of Fairfax Court House. They trampled underfoot the remnants of paper and broken glass from last night, marching toward Centreville and the enemy. At one point they marched past a supply wagon travelling at a slower pace. Tethered to the back was a slow-moving cow plodding mournfully along. The wagon was filled with sheep, pigs, crates of chickens, and a new-born calf with black spotted eye and a black tail. Charley froze for an instant until pushed ahead by Hans behind him. He lost the cadence of his drum beat. That had to be Bessie and her calf! How dare those wild, thieving soldiers take them from Horace and his grandmother. Charley motioned in horror to Frank as if they should or could do something about it. But Frank, who obviously had seen also, thrust his head down and kept his eyes forward.

By mid-day Charley was moving automatically forward, daydreaming of home, Grandpa Eb, and Elspeth. He was startled by the sudden cheering of the troops in the columns ahead. As he marched on, the sound grew louder. Rounding a bend in the road, a cheer broke from his own throat when he saw the stars and stripes snapping crisply in the breeze, flying high above what had been the enemy camp! The fifers spontaneously struck up "Rally Round the Flag." Charley beat the rhythm, and the marching men began to sing. Company F entered the center of the abandoned Rebel camp amid music and cheers.

Large log huts stood row upon row, already occupied by the Union troops which had arrived earlier. Captain Sweeney directed the company to the area assigned to their regiment. After conferring with the captain, Sergeant O'Toole pointed to a large central hut with wood stacked neatly by the door, and said, "Here, lads, is home sweet home. All the comforts your mamas provided for ya. Stash your packs, get some grub, and rest up. There'll be work enough later."

All twelve boys of the drum corps were able to fit comfort-ably into the large structure. Two stone fireplaces, one at each end, were soon ablaze. A rough table and benches were in the center of the room, and a wooden floor provided a warm, dry space for bed rolls.

Not only was a supply of dry firewood left beside each fireplace, but good rations of food stood untouched, as well as many items of interest made by the Rebs over the long winter months. Charley found a corn cob doll with corn silk hair exactly the shade of Elspeth's. He put it in his backpack and thought how pleased she would be when he gave it to her. A wooden jigsaw puzzle was perfect for his little brothers and a dancing man on a paddle for his sisters. As he packed the items to mail home, Charley thought of the Reb's hands which carved them. Was he an older man with children at home? Maybe he was a young person like himself who made the toys to send to younger brothers and sisters.

The drummer boys did not get outside the camp during the next few days, but they heard talk of the damage done by the retreating Rebs. The Manassas railroad tracks were twisted as though by the hands of a giant, and the charred depot and steam engine were still smoldering.

"I thought we were gonna see some Rebs," Hans said at supper that night. "But all we see are the old logs painted to look like guns. Huh, must be some fighters if all they do is make false guns."

"Well, Quaker guns are all right with me. Nice and peaceable, and they don't make any noise to scare the horses!" laughed Jacob Adams.

"They sure left us some good food, though, if this is any sample," Patrick added as he scraped the last of his beef stew from his tin dish.

"Yeah, but they didn't leave us any railroad to ride on," said Charley. "Looks like we have to chase the Rebs south on foot."

"But when?" Frank asked. "Seems like we wait, quick march, then wait again. It's gettin' downright boring."

Finally on the 15th of March, the restless soldiers received orders to move back to Alexandria. Instead of following the

Rebs by foot toward Richmond, they were to be moved by boats
down the Potomac and the Chesapeake Bay to Norfolk, where
they could begin a land march to Richmond. Excitement filled
the camp as the troops stood at attention on the parade ground
to hear an address from General McClellan, the beloved "Little
Mac," read aloud by the major.

"Look at him," whispered Frank to Charley. "Hair prettier
than a girl's!" The major stood on a platform, golden shoulder-
length hair slightly blowing in the breeze.

Charley said, "I wonder who polished his boots for him."

The boys snickered, but when he started to read the words
of General McClellan in his rich baritone voice, all thoughts of
the pompous major disappeared . . . "I am to watch over you
as a parent over his children; and you know that your general
loves you from the depths of his heart. It shall be my care, as it
has ever been, to gain success with the least possible loss, but I
know that, if it is necessary, you will willingly follow me to your
graves for our righteous cause . . . . I shall demand of you great,
heroic exertions, rapid and long marches, desperate combats,
privations perhaps. We will share all these together; and when
this sad war is over we will return to our homes, and feel that
we can ask no higher honor than the proud consciousness that
we belonged to the Army of the Potomac."

Chapter Six

Marching down the narrow streets of Alexandria soon became impossible. The Pennsylvania 49th was engulfed in a large crowd of men, moving slowly toward the waterfront. Zouaves in white leggings and red baggy trousers, teamsters leading mules, and blue tunics as far as Charley could see in front and behind him. He could do nothing but inch forward.

"Stay together, lads," O'Toole's voice came from somewhere up ahead, but Charley could not see beyond the backs of the men in front. He tried to protect his drum from being crushed when a mule skinner, cursing and shouting at his charges, forced his way through. As the crowd separated, he saw Frank, Patrick, and Sergeant O'Toole briefly before they were gone. He raised his hand in hopes they would see him, but it was too late. His foot slipped in the droppings left by the mules, and he was down before he knew it. All he could see were boots and blue legs. His drumsticks rolled on the cobbles. Men cursed and tried to jump over him. As he was trying to pick himself up, he was pushed down again by the crowd who could not see a young boy crouched on the street with his arms now protectively over his head. Suddenly he felt strong arms pull him to his feet as he grasped desperately for his drum.

"Well now, this isn't any way to fight a war, young Charley," Jacob Adams said, as he steadied him and then placed a protective arm around him as they moved forward.

At the waterfront, the crowd of men in blue thinned and suddenly Charley saw spread before him all the hub-bub and activity of a busy port. Charley had never been to a port city before. The sight of steamers, tall schooners, and low, flat barges massed at the docks, and still others spread across the wide river awaiting their turns was exhilarating. Charley, Patrick, Hans, and Frank had made their way to the very edge of the docks and finally were seated to the side of one long wharf, their legs dangling toward the murky water.

"Are you sure Sergeant O'Toole said our embarkation orders are for tomorrow?" Patrick asked. "All this noise and confusion makes me nervous. How are we going to find our way back to the company?"

"I'm sure!" Frank said angrily. "You've asked us that four times already!"

"Yeah," added Hans. "Sergeant O'Toole told us to meet him under the clock tower at 6:00. Let's take advantage of our freedom for a change."

Charley sat silently in awe of the entire situation, hardly believing that all these men, animals, and wagon upon wagon of stores, equipment, rations, and ammunition could ever be loaded onto this vast variety of boats! The wooden decks visibly settled lower and lower into the water as boxes of cartridges were piled on.

"I don't know about you," said Patrick, "but I hope we're not put on one of them schooners. They look so tippy and there ain't much to them."

"Give me one of the steamers," said Frank. "I ain't sleepin' below the water level. I wanna look out and see light and breathe air."

"I don't think we'll have any choice," Charley said. "We'll be packed in like tinned sardines any way you look at it, but those schooners with their sails filled with wind must move smooth and silent down the river. Look at that one, 'The White Lady.' It says Portland, Maine on the side. I wonder how long it took to sail itself here."

The game of identifying the home ports of the different ships occupied the boys—a schooner from Boston, a steamer from New York City, a barge from Delaware.

Patrick pointed to a large ship maneuvering its way around smaller vessels toward the wharf, "Look, a home ship, 'Liberty,' from Philadelphia, Pennsylvania. That's ours for sure!"

"Well, wherever ours comes from, I sure hope it has a place to sit softer than this wharf," Charley said as he stood, rubbing his backside.

"Here come some of your friends; you smell just like them." Frank laughed at Charley, as a man with a long whip cracking moved six pack mules down the wharf to a waiting barge. The mules brayed and flattened long ears back against their heads in a useless attempt to escape the sound of the mule skinner's whip and cursing. The boys watched as the mules were led and pushed and cajoled down the narrow plank onto the barge.

"Now, my pretty, that's good, straight ahead now." "You great ugly brute, git, or I'll skin you alive!" The mule skinner switched between sweet talk and threats as the animals first shied away and then, in spite of themselves, complied. As the six mules brayed and stomped, the handler and his deck hands moved quickly, bending low to the animals' legs to chain the mules together. Before the chains could be secured to the iron rings on the deck of the barge, the front mule reared up, kicking out at the skinner. The others reacted similarly and before anything could be done, the first mule was over the low edge of the barge and into the water! The chain clanked as it raked across the side of the barge. The mule skinner jumped to his feet shouting, "Release the chain! Release the chain!" But the other men knew that it was hopeless and stepped away from the flaying hooves and chains. They watched, open mouthed, as one by one the mules dragged each other into the deep water. The terrified screams of the animals were almost human. The boys and men alike were sickened by the sound and the sight as they stood by helplessly. The water was white with froth where the animals kicked and screamed. Finally there was silence, and the water was calm as if nothing had ever happened. The mule skinner slumped upon the deck of the barge, staring at the spot in the water where his animals had drowned, as if he hoped that somehow they would reappear.

The boys stood silently. Then, as if of one thought, they turned and started walking away from the waterfront.

At the cold, clear dawn of the next morning, Charley found himself back on the same wharf, this time massed with the entire 49th Pennsylvania Regiment. As the sun slipped above the trees, sending fingers of bright light across the river, Charley beat his drum in rhythm as the band played "Battle Cry of Freedom." Company F marched smartly up the gangplank with burnished steel gun barrels flashing in the bright welcoming warmth of the sun and regimental flags snapping in the breeze. Charley felt a fierce swelling pride for the Union.

As quickly as possible the boys found a spot to stow their gear and then made their way back to the railings to watch the loading of the other steamers. The boys laughed and punched each other as they tried to gain balance when the deck shifted under their feet.

"You fellas are land-lubbers for sure," Patrick said. "Look, like this." He spread his feet apart and bent his knees slightly. "That's how you do it."

"What makes you such an all-fired expert?" Frank asked.

"Aw, my pa and me, we go fishin' all the time. It's easy, you'll see. We ain't even left port yet. Wait till we get down to the bay. Better practice now."

Eventually when the sun had moved higher still into the sky, the flagship gave its signal, and the entire heavily laden flotilla moved out into the river. The deck shuddered as the ship got up steam. Charley felt the vibration go through his body as his hands gripped the wooden rail. The engine roared, drowning out the sound of the bands playing on the docks and the people cheering and waving hats and scarves in the air. It all looked like a pantomime—no sound but the pounding engine. Charley noticed one of the young women on the shore who wore a calico dress the same color as Elspeth's.

As the steamer passed the navy yard, a salute was fired, and the boys took off their hats and waved wildly back at the men on shore. Many of the soldiers took advantage of their idle time and, having rolled out their bed rolls, immediately were lulled into naps by the drone of the engines and the slight roll of the deck. Not Charley. He and Patrick remained glued to the rail, watching every inch of shoreline that slipped by. And when another salute was fired in honor of the flotilla as they rounded the point guarded by Fort Washington, the boys again waved their hats and cheered.

Mount Vernon swept into view, and the bells of the entire fleet tolled in memory of President George Washington. Charley and Patrick, joined again at the railing by Frank and Hans, stood in awe of the mansion and its lovely, broad expanse of lawn just turning green in the early spring.

Jacob Adams laid his arm across Charley's shoulders and with his other hand pointed out a clump of firs. "Do you see that, just south and a little below the house? There lies the tomb of the father of our country. What must his spirit be thinking of us now, trying to hold together the country he founded?"

Charley wondered what his mama and papa would think of this scene. He decided that he must remember the details so at the first opportunity he could describe everything in a letter home.

After the grand sight of Mount Vernon, the others lost interest in the scenery and went to find card games, or, grumbling about the lack of good food, went to chew on some hardtack biscuits. But Charley still stood by the rail for glimpses of another mansion here and there. Occasionally they passed a few lesser homes surrounded by land painstakingly cultivated by lone farmers. Charley waved at one man who stood in a muddy field behind his plow. After a few moments, the man raised his arm in acknowledgement. Was he a Rebel or a Yank? Charley wondered.

When finally the heavily forested shoreline became monotonous, Charley shifted his attention. As he looked around, he could see only ships as far behind him as ahead, their decks black with men. The flotilla moved resolutely through the water, a giant crocodile of men, animals, and weapons, swiftly and steadily advancing to devour the enemy.

Sometime during the night the gentle swing of the hammock became so strong that Charley was awakened when he hit the side of the bulkhead with a thud. The *Liberty* was decidedly pitching. All around him men, who were crowded into tight sleeping quarters, were awakened and grumbling. Soon the smell of those who became sick from the ship's motion made it impossible to remain below deck. Once in the fresh air, he stood trying to balance himself. Remembering what Patrick had said, he bent his knees slightly and walked or lunged toward the rail. Charley was surprised to see that he was not the only "land-lubber" seeking some fresh air. The ship's rail was lined with the dark forms of men.

"Sure smells like a river bed at low tide down there," someone said.

"Where are we?" asked another.

"Out in the broad Chesapeake," came the answer from one of the dark forms.

Charley could just make out the dim outline of the ships nearest the *Liberty*, their red and green port and starboard oil lamps disappearing and reappearing as the ships bobbed in the swells of the bay. In the distance an occasional light on shore pierced the darkness.

At dawn, the shoreline gradually became visible—gray and misty. The flag flying over Fort Monroe was outlined against the sky. The *Liberty* dropped anchor to await the signal of the harbor master to dock.

"One of the strongest fortifications in the Union and one the Rebs haven't been able to get, even though we're in Dixie now," said one of the soldiers of the 49th.

"Sure looks big," Charley said. "Wonder how long we'll stay here?"

"Not long, if I know anything. Why, we'll be up to take Richmond in no time," he answered.

Charley heard much laughter from the other side of the boat and went over to find out what was so amusing. Hans and Frank were bent double with laughter and pointed speechlessly at a strange object in the water.

"Must be a sea monster," someone said.

"Or a floating bucket," another added.

Hans said, "It looks like a whale floating just below the water."

"Ya ever see a whale with a man walking on its back?" Frank said. "Don't be stupid."

An ironclad boat with a round wooden deck on top lay in the water of the bay. An officer with a spy glass directed toward Hampton Roads and the James River paced the small deck.

"What is it?" asked Charley in wonder.

"It's the *Monitor*," answered one of the men. "Our brave little ironclad *Mistress of the Seas*. She's on the lookout for another encounter with the *Merrimack*."

"Let her show herself in these waters now and she won't last long!"

"It's a funny feeling to know that a Reb ship with guns is lurking around here someplace," Patrick said as they all sat down to drink the strong hot coffee and to chew on their hardtack breakfast.

"Maybe we'll get to see a real navy battle," Charley said.

"Yeah, but I'd rather watch from shore than out here in the bay," Hans added.

The morning had turned damp and cold, a wet mist settling on everything and everyone on deck. The boys still preferred the open air to the close quarters and smells below deck. The *Liberty* bobbed at anchor awaiting orders to dock and disembark. In the mass confusion, countless other ships slipped in ahead. Finally, in his frustration, the captain shouted, "It's everyone for himself, forge ahead!" And the *Liberty* with its powerful engines forced its way into the dock. Now the job of unloading men and supplies began. In the excitement the boys soon forgot the hoped-for second battle between the two great ironclads, the Union's *Monitor* and the Confederates' *Merrimack*.

The scene on shore was one of even grander confusion than the embarkation in Alexandria. Masses of infantry, long trains of artillery, thousands of cavalry were all mingled with army wagons, neighing horses, and braying mules. It was amazing to Charley that regiments managed to stay together and make their way to the fields beyond Hampton to lay down their packs, stack their arms, and pitch their tents.

In surrounding fields the boys watched regiments which had arrived on earlier flotillas enact mock battles. Here was a line, nearly a mile long, of soldiers kneeling like statues with presented bayonets as if awaiting a dash of enemy cavalry. There in a second field was another brigade with fixed bayonets actually charging the invisible enemy. Cavalry, with plumed hats and sabers drawn, raced across a field. In still another field artillery caissons pulled by teams of six horses, with one rider for each two horses, raced into position and unharnessed the horses. Other soldiers primed the big guns to simulate firing. Then, harnessing the horses again, the whole procedure was repeated. The sounds of horses whinnying, men shouting orders, and heavy artillery being pulled were new to the boys.

For nearly two weeks the Pennsylvania 49th camped in the fields around Hampton, providing an opportunity for the mail to catch up with the troops. The soldiers, hungry for news from home, eagerly seized letters and packets when their names were called out.

Charley was surprised to receive several letters, two from West Chester and one from Lewinsville, Virginia. He opened the one from Elspeth first and was delighted to see two pages written in a precise and clear hand. She wrote of life on the farm and everyday matters. "Life is quiet around Lewinsville since the troops have moved out. I have the little carving you made for me on the window sill in my room." Charley smiled at the memory of the mule, Nelson, he had whittled for her, but then the letter took a turn which worried him. "Things are hard here," she wrote. "The land is overworked and everything is too dear. Papa is talking about moving on to western territory to homestead with his brother." Charley felt his throat go dry. Western territory, where, when? If the Sinclairs move before the war is over, how would he ever find his friend again?

New flotillas arrived daily off Fort Monroe, delivering thousands more men and supplies. Each day seemed to bring another glorious parade of infantry, cavalry, and artillery as the men ran through their exercises. Finally on April 2, rumor had it that "Little Mac" had arrived, and on the morning of April 4, the Pennsylvania 49th was on the move again.

Chapter Seven

Siege of Yorktown, Virginia —— April, 1862

Charley found himself trudging along in the midst of a huge cavalcade. The countryside was so different from his Pennsylvania home and even the area around Washington! Here the flat land was dotted with worn-out fields, marshes, and thick pine forests. Every now and then they saw forlorn Negro families who had piled into wagons or were huddled along the roadside as the soldiers passed. Charley looked into the eyes of a boy about his own age and gave him a quick smile. The dark eyes in the dark face looked back distrustfully.

At noon when the troops rested, chewing on their salt pork rations, Sergeant O'Toole plopped down on the ground among the drummer boys and leaned his broad back against a pine tree. "Ya ask these colored folk a question and either they play dumb or they talk your ear off, and I can't understand half of what they say. Their masters have left, their masters are here to defend their homes, the Rebs have retreated, the Rebs are hiding all around in the woods. Who knows what to believe? I think they'll say anything they think we want to hear."

"Maybe we scare them marching through with all our guns and drums," Charley said.

"Humph," O'Toole grumped as he stood and brushed the mud from the seat of his trousers. "Sure, folks around here better be gettin' used ta us. We'll be here for a bit o'time."

During the afternoon, intermittent rains turned the low-lying woods and roads into lakes and mires.

"This mud will suck the boots right off your feet," Patrick said as he struggled to move forward.

Charley just grunted in response. He was too busy trying to lift each foot to answer.

"Yeah, runt. Don't fall in or we'll never find you," Frank growled.

Men, boys, even officers began to discard some of their heavy belongings, such as blankets, parade coats, and extra shoes. The roadside was littered with the discarded items.

"But we'll need our blankets tonight," Charley protested when Frank was the first of the drum corps to toss his aside.

"Sure, nitwit. But then we just pick another one up when we want it."

It made sense when Charley looked at the long line ahead, so he too cast his to the road.

"What's the hold up ahead?" someone behind Charley shouted when the column of men came to an abrupt halt.

"Wagon's stuck. Can't be moved by man nor mule," came the reply from the front of the column. The word was passed back. "Wagon stuck." "Wagon up to axles in mud." "Wagon mired, can't move."

"King, Simpson, Lynch, and Schmidt!" Captain Sweeney shouted. "I want you to go with Corporal Adams and Private Young and cut some saplings for a road bed. We've got to move these wagons and guns. Adams, you and Young stand guard while these lads cut. Don't know if Rebs are in the woods or not."

As Jacob Adams led the small band, Charley asked, "How will the trees help to move the wagons?"

"We'll make a corduroy road, lads, just lay the saplings down crosswise on the mud, and it's like Pennsylvania Avenue. We'll just roll right on."

All around them men were sawing or cutting, then hacking the branches from the small trees.

"Pile them up here, boys. No, no, that one's too big. No wider than about five or six inches, I said," shouted the captain of the Engineering Corps, who was in charge.

The line of men passed the logs out to the road in a bucket brigade formation, and others laid them one after another across the muddy ruts. Finally, standing in mud which was knee deep, Charley looked in wonder as the wagons and cannons bumped slowly but surely over the newly laid corduroy road.

"Don't think I've ever been so tired," Patrick said as he extricated one foot from the mud and joined the column of men following the wagons in a snail-like procession.

"Yeah, but look at this road," said Frank. "Wouldn't be here without us!"

The corps continued the monotonous march until they were startled by a loud boom and cracking sounds as something whizzed through tree branches and eventually landed harmlessly in the woods to their left. Horses plodding along the road pulling the wagons, reared and whinnied, eyes wide with fright as a deafening volley of artillery exploded.

"Get down!" a voice from the rear shouted. Charley and the others were pushed or fell forward onto the rough logs of the corduroy road.

"Look out! Rebs got cannon up ahead! Drummers to the rear!" Orders were barked out by Sergeant O'Toole. Charley and the other drummers ran to the rear of the column, hunched over and heads down as if running through a pelting rain.

A second volley of explosions sounded as the Pennsylvania 49th spread out through the woods. The drummers beat a steady rhythm as the men advanced toward a marshy creek where the unseen enemy was entrenched on the opposite bank.

The shots ceased as suddenly as they had started. Charley's heart continued to pound. He, Frank, Patrick, and Hans all looked at each other with panic-stricken faces and then looked away as if ashamed to show their fright. Charley's eyes scanned the woods. He wondered where the next shots would come from and where there might be some shelter, but nothing happened.

The silence stretched on, and then the men of the regiment began to pick up their packs and haversacks and shoulder their weapons. Orders were to continue their march toward Yorktown. But now they paralleled Warwick Creek, and although they were concealed from view by the thick pine forest, they were intensely aware of the nearby presence of the enemy.

Charley kept his eyes on the woods to his left as he marched, afraid of seeing the enemy, but at the same time afraid to look away. Then through a small clearing in the trees across the creek, Charley saw the enemy for the first time. He gulped hard as he glimpsed mounted Rebel troops thundering through the woods toward Yorktown.

"Sure is quiet now," Frank said in a low voice. "We know the Rebs are over there. Why don't they shoot?"

"I don' t know," Charley said. "But if you look through those trees across the creek, sometimes you can see the Rebs. Why, there must be thousands of them."

The army camped in the woods along the creek that night. Every so often the Rebs and the guards on picket duty exchanged gunfire. Charley was curled up in his bed roll near the foot of a large pine tree where soft pine needles provided some relief to his aching muscles. The sound of rifle shot awoke him. He pressed his back closer to the tree trunk and stared into the night trying not to breathe too loudly. Where were the Rebs? Were they creeping closer in the darkness, surrounding them? He could not keep himself from thinking of home, his warm bed, the voices of his brothers and sisters, the smell of his mama's cooking, and the bright kitchen fire. He longed to be there again.

Early the next morning the regiment was marching. Charley felt as if he had not slept at all, and his muscles ached with every movement. Approaching Yorktown through rain and ever-present mud, Charley's heart pounded in fearful anticipation as he heard the enemy's artillery grow louder.

"Can hear those Reb cannons for sure now," said Patrick.

"I don't care," said Hans. "Just want to pitch a tent, get out of the awful rain, and sleep! No cannon fire's gonna keep me awake, less it's shootin' right at me."

Charley pulled his oilskin higher around the back of his neck, but it was useless against the relentless rain. "I sure hope we can find some high ground, or at least a dry field to camp tonight," he said. "That last stream we crossed was waist-high."

"Sure, waist-high for you, shrimp, but knee-high for the rest of us." Frank's attempt at humor was ignored. The effort of just putting one foot in front of the other and moving forward took all their energy.

Within three miles of Yorktown, the gunfire had stopped. The other troops, which had arrived ahead of them, were already busily digging earthworks as if for a siege. The Pennsylvania 49th pitched camp.

Three days later Charley settled himself comfortably into one of the newly reinforced earthworks to write a letter home. The ground was still damp, but the rain had stopped for the last day and a half. He had spread his blankets and tunic over some branches to dry. Now, bareheaded and in his shirt sleeves, he relaxed in the warmth of the sun.

Yorktown, VA. April, 1862

My Dear Mama and Papa,

Your most welcome letter found me at Fortress Monroe after our regiment was shipped down the Potomac River and the Chesapeake Bay. I cannot fully describe to you the excitement of the journey with all the ships and supplies and multitudes of regiments. I will have much to tell you when I return home. On our march toward Yorktown, we came under shot and shell, but with no casualties. We drummer boys were quickly ordered to the rear of the company while our brave men prepared to return the enemy's fire.

By day we are digging new and reinforcing some old earthworks still remaining here from our War of

Independence. The ground is soft due to the many days of rain, and the men complain bitterly of the mud slides and slow progress. I spent my thirteenth birthday busy searching for dry wood for the fires. Forests are all around us, but very little dry kindling is to be found. How nice it would be to have a pile of clean, dry wood as you have just outside the kitchen door, Mama. I hope Willy keeps the wood box full for you in my absence.

I was happy to learn that your business is so prosperous, Papa. You must feel very proud that you are providing uniforms for our army. My own uniform trousers are now above my ankles. I guess I have grown some since leaving home. Mama, do not despair that I am neglectful of my religious duties. For when we are encamped, as we are now, Chaplain Rutherford holds services every evening.

Tell Theo that I often see a great yellow balloon rise above the camps. The balloon is fastened to the ground by cables. From the basket which hangs beneath the balloon, the aeronaut can view with his spyglass all the enemy camps and movements.

I must return to duty now. Please write again soon.

Your loving son,
Charles King

Several days later in the hour before dawn when the clear sky was taking on a rosy glow, Charley stood at attention awaiting orders to sound roll call. An officer, accompanied by his aide, rode through camp, perched high on his horse. A sword hung smartly at his left side, gold fringed epaulets adorned the blue tunic, and red plumes festooned his hat.

Patrick nudged Charley and whispered, "Must be some fancy general to dress like that. Look at those turkey feathers!"

They watched silently as the officer approached in all his splendor and were surprised when he stopped in front of them.

The general looked each of them up and down and spoke quietly to his aide. Then, speaking directly to Charley, he asked, "Have you had the schooling to write properly, son?"

Charley stared up at the general for a moment until nudged again by Patrick. "Yes, sir," he replied.

"Fine!" the general said with a grin. "Son, you're about to have a great adventure." And, again with an aside to his aide, he trotted off. Before Charley knew what was happening, his drum was taken from him, and in one motion he was swept up onto the horse to ride behind the general's aide. Stunned by what was happening, Charley looked down at the other boys. Even Sergeant O'Toole stood there in silent surprise. Then, as the horse moved forward, Charley gripped the belt of the man in front.

"Don't be alarmed, son," he said. "Here's one time it's good luck to be small. The general wants to observe the enemy from his balloon, and he wants to do it right away. He needs a light-weight note taker, and you're just right for the job. For once you can look down on the world."

When they reached the open field, Charley saw the beplumed general striding around a partially inflated balloon, shouting orders. Men ran around pumping gas into the huge yellow ball. The canvas made a sharp cracking sound like a rifle shot, as each fold snapped full. Charley watched the big black letters, printed on the canvas, appear. Crack . . . I . . . Crack . . . N . . . Crack . . . T . . . until the balloon was nearly full, and the word INTREPID was plainly showing.

The aide thrust a writing tablet and graphite pencil into his hand and lifted Charley into the basket with a smile of encouragement. Charley squeezed himself back against the side to make room for the general as he leaped in and shouted, "Now, men! With all speed! Let out the cables!"

Scurrying around the balloon, the ground crew worked the cable fastened to the great yellow mass. Not yet fully inflated, the balloon rose fitfully, the basket swinging, rocking, and tilting dangerously to the side.

A shout from the ground crew reached them, "Only one cable secured, sir!"

"Carry on," was the general's reply.

Charley dropped his writing tablet to the floor and held on to the side of the basket. Swaying side to side, he watched the men below become smaller and smaller. His stomach turned over, and he hoped he would not vomit. Higher and higher they went until suddenly the balloon stopped with a jerk as they reached the end of the cable.

The general drew a long spyglass from inside his tunic, and standing, legs spread for balance, he turned his glass on the enemy encampment surrounding Yorktown. As he scanned the area, he spoke, "I was in all haste to ascend because it is imperative that I view the enemy position in the clear air of predawn. Any change in the number of campfires can give us information of enemy troop movements faster than any other source. . . . Ah, just as I thought, a new encampment there to the east, along the York River. Do you have that, son?"

Charley gripped the pencil in his nearly numb fingers and struggled to write legibly in spite of the movement of the basket and his shivering body. A loud crack sounded, and suddenly the *Intrepid* rose rapidly! The single, strained cable which had held her steady at 300 feet had snapped! Shouts of alarm were heard from below. Tablet and pencil forgotten, Charley clung to the rim of the basket in terror.

The general swore loudly and, leaning over the edge causing the basket to tilt dangerously, he waved his arms and shouted to the unhearing ears below, "You incompetent idiots! How in blazes did you let this happen?" Then more calmly, "WHAT . . . ARE . . . MY . . . INSTRUCTIONS?"

Charley saw the small figures below break into a helpless frenzy as the balloon continued to rise with the fragment of the rotted cable trailing wildly. In spite of his dangerous situation, all he could think of was an ant hill which had just been poked with a stick. Movement began over the entire Union camp as the men learned of their predicament. Directly below at the launching field,

Professor Lowe himself shouted orders, and Charley was amazed that he could hear the shrill voice rise so clearly through the air. He was saying, "OPEN . . . THE . . . VALVE. . . . CLIMB . . . TO . . . THE . . . NETTING . . . AND . . . REACH . . . THE . . . VALVE . . . ROPE!"

A multitude of men took up the shout, "THE VALVE! THE VALVE!"

Charley watched the entire scene, not so much in terror or even as an active participant, but more as if standing outside himself. The general laid his spyglass and plumed hat in the bottom of the basket and said to Charley, "Huddle low, son. I don't want you falling out of this car."

Then he began to climb the netting, slowly and precariously. He stretched to his full height, arm extended, and tried repeatedly to grab the wildly blowing valve rope. But at each attempt the wind tossed the rope just beyond his grasp, and when he nearly lost his footing, he descended to the basket.

"It's no use in this wind, son. We'll attempt it again in a calm." And then with a smile of encouragement and a pat on Charley's shoulder, he said, "Let's make the most of this situation and do what we came to do. We'll be a true spectacle for all below." He handed Charley the tablet and pencil, then picked up his spyglass and placed his hat back on his head.

Charley managed a smile in return. "Yes, sir," he said. He looked below at the swarm of men still moving like an army of ants as the balloon moved fitfully in different directions. When the general put his spyglass to his eye, a roar of laughter arose, followed by applause from their grand audience. Charley could not help laughing aloud himself.

Suddenly the balloon slowed and faltered, then changed direction. With another great gust of south wind, the balloon moved toward the enemy. Cheers from the ground changed to howls of despair as the small army of two drifted over the Confederate line. The wind swept the general's hat from his head. It swooped and whirled as currents grabbed it, tossed it, and dropped it further. Confederate sharpshooters fired at it repeatedly, until the hat dropped to the ground, shot through. Dislodged plumes drifted and fluttered like a flock of red birds.

The balloon moved steadily on over sharpshooters, rifle pits, the outer works, and then the actual ramparts and cannons, and the town itself. Charley wrote furiously as the general rattled off numbers and terms Charley didn't even understand. At one point the general said, "Don't fear the big guns, son. They cannot be brought to bear upon the balloon. And we are above range of the sharpshooters." And at another point, he leaned back and sighed. "Ah, what a grand view, and oh what you and I shall speak of to our children and grandchildren some day."

"They've stopped shooting, sir," said Charley. The guns and shouts had ceased, as men on both sides gazed skyward in rapt anticipation. Now the rush of air around the small basket and the large balloon was the only sound as the general continued to observe the enemy below.

"Yes, and now that the sun is high in the sky, we must watch for an opportunity to take things in hand."

As though responding to the general's statement, the *Intrepid* plunged, tacked, veered, and drifted rapidly back toward the Federal lines and safety.

"It's now or never, young man. Are you keen?"

"Yes, sir," replied Charley, though he had no idea of the general's plans.

"Good. As soon as we are back over friendly lines, I will hoist you up on my shoulders to reach the valve rope. Pull it with all your might!"

"Yes, sir," Charley answered again, a little less assuredly.

They both watched the land below. When they had finally drifted over a field scattered with Federal tents, the general squatted low in the basket. Charley climbed onto his shoulders, and the general, with a firm grip on Charley's legs, stood to his full height. Charley stretched as far as he could, but was still a good two feet away from the dangling rope.

"All right, son. Get a good grip on the netting and pull yourself to a standing position. Don't fear. I'll keep hold of your feet."

Charley fought the instinctive urge to crawl back to the safety of the basket. He reached out to the netting and slowly, gingerly, pulled himself upward until his feet were on the general's shoulders. The wind scooped his hat from his head and sent it sailing away. As he watched the path of his hat, he froze in panic. Nothing but vast space and the sound of the wind surrounded him.

"Don't look down!" shouted the general.

Charley obeyed, squeezed his eyes shut for a moment, and hoped that his stomach would go back where it belonged.

"Almost there!" shouted the general, as Charley freed one hand from the netting and extended it toward the swinging valve rope. The tip brushed his fingers, but was blown from his grasp.

"Just a little further now. Don't worry, I've got you." The general's strong hands gripped his ankles as Charley stretched again and again.

"I can't!" he shouted. "I can't!"

"Yes, you can, son! Just a bit more!"

Charley took a deep breath and stretched as far as he could. He nearly lost his hold on the netting with his other hand.

"Now, son, now!" And Charley had the valve rope in his hand.

"Pull! Pull!" the general shouted.

Charley pulled, and immediately the balloon began its plunge to the earth like a stone, as the gas was released. Charley and the general together were thrown to the bottom of the basket.

"Brace yourself like so," said the general as he placed his feet against the opposite side and tucked his head down, covering his neck with his arms. Charley barely had time to follow his instructions, so fast was their descent and so terrifying was the blood pounding in his temples.

With a great and final thud they landed. All the wind was knocked from Charley, and he could not move as folds and folds of oiled canvas fell over them. He did not know at first where he was or if he was hurt. Somehow the general was on his feet and out of the basket, but Charley huddled there stunned until the canvas covering him was parted. A large hand reached down toward him, and grasping it, he was suddenly pulled into the daylight by the general.

He smiled at Charley and said, "Well, son, I promised you adventure. How does it feel to be an aeronaut?"

In his confusion, Charley could not think what to say. Everything was happening so fast! The entire Federal army seemed to be racing toward them, the general's personal staff galloping up on horseback. And from out of nowhere a band began to play amid cheers from all the men. Everyone was so concerned for the safety of the general that Charley was forgotten. The general, assuring his staff that he was completely unharmed and perfectly fit, mounted his horse. He turned to Charley, giving him a quick smile and a brisk salute. Charley stood next to the collapsed *Intrepid* and watched the general ride away.

Chapter Eight

Yorktown, Virginia —— April and May, 1862

All eyes were on Charley that night as the men sat around the campfire. "Tell us, what is it like to be a bird and fly above all?" one asked. Then, "Yeah," chimed in another, "do things look the same? Can you see the people below?"

"It was sure a sight to behold—that great yellow ball with the sun shining through it and you, a little black ant, crawling up the rigging to pull that rope!" said Patrick. "Were you scared?"

"Well, yes," said Charley, although now the terror was nearly forgotten he wallowed in all the attention. He took a sip of coffee, then dipping his hard biscuit into the hot brew, he watched as meal worms emerged from the biscuit. They wriggled desperately for a few seconds, then were still, floating atop the hot liquid. In revulsion, Charley threw coffee and biscuit into the fire.

"Well, are you going to tell us what it was like?" prompted Frank.

"I don't know what it was like, except that it was cold, and the wind howled, and I was afraid that the basket would tip over at any minute. And it was beautiful and . . . and free. I could see for miles . . . when I wasn't taking notes, that is."

"And when you landed on that tent, it collapsed as though struck by lightning!"

Charley had not been aware of that. "I hope no one was sleeping in it!" he said.

"No chance! Every man in the entire army was outside watching the spectacle!" said Frank.

"We all saw, when you went skippin' up the riggin', 'twas a brave thing ya did, boy-O," said Sergeant O'Toole. "Now lads, there's already been a skirmish near here. And we sent the enemy skidaddling, but there's more to come, so turn in and rest while ya can."

"First, give us a tune, Jacob."

Jacob Adams sat up and stretched. "I've already put my fiddle to bed, but in honor of our flying drummer boy . . ." Effortlessly he began to sing,

> Oh mother, how pretty the moon looks tonight;
> 'Twas never so cunning before.
> Its two little arms are so sharp and so bright;
> I hope they won' t grow anymore.

A harmonica joined in.

> If I were up there with you by my side;
> We' d rock in it nicely you'd see.
> We'd sit in the middle and hold by both ends.
> And on the next rainbow come home.

> We'd call to the stars to keep out of our way;
> Lest we should rock over their toes.
> And there we would stay till the end of the day
> And on the next rainbow come home.

Charley looked at the night sky. He thought, "I was really up there, floating on the air. I was part of the sky!"

Jacob's strong voice faded as the tune ended, "And on the next rainbow come home."

The boys and men of Company F wandered from the campfire a few at a time. Charley, still excited by all the day's activity, lingered along with Jacob Adams and O'Toole, quietly watching the flames.

"You surely have something to write the folks about now," Jacob Adams said, emptying his pipe into the fire.

"Yes, that's true," a voice said. All three turned, surprised at the sound. All they could see were the boots within the light thrown by the fire. The speaker remained in darkness. "But we don't want to alarm the folks at home, do we?" Captain Sweeney said, as he moved forward into the light.

All three started to scramble to their feet in the presence of an officer. "Stay as you are," he said. "I just wanted to stop by to congratulate you, Drummer King, on your fine work today."

"Thank you, sir."

"You can't keep a Pennsylvania boy down," Sweeney chuckled at his own joke as he sat down cross-legged next to Charley. "But you must realize that the home folks, good as they are, don't understand all we fighting men go through. And there's no need upsetting them now, is there?"

"No sir, I guess not," Charley responded.

Jacob Adams and Sergeant O'Toole spoke to each other in low tones so as to appear disinterested in what the captain was saying. But at the same time, they strained to hear everything.

"Good man," said Captain Sweeney. "Just so we understand each other." As he rose and brushed off his uniform, Sweeney held out his hand in a signal for the others not to rise and said again to Charley, "Good work, King, good work." He strode off into the darkness.

"Well, now, I wonder what all the sudden attention to the peace of mind of the home folks is all about," Jacob Adams said to Sergeant O'Toole.

"Ah sure, maybe Sweeney has taken up home health care as a sideline," O'Toole responded as he smiled and leaned back on his elbow, crossing one leg over the other. "Or maybe Mr. Drummer Charles King can enlighten us."

"Well," said Charley, "I think it's because Captain Sweeney asked my folks a few times if I could join up with the 49th. And he promised that I would be safe if they said yes."

Both O'Toole and Adams threw their heads back and laughed and laughed. Charley joined in the laughter although he did not fully catch the joke.

"I swear, lad, you're full a' more surprises than a barrel a' monkeys. Safe is it? Flyin' around with the birds and bein' shot at from below! Oh yeah, safe!" And again all three laughed.

Charley found some free time to write letters home, and although he was told not to tell his family about the balloon flight, he took great pride in describing his adventure in the runaway *Intrepid* to Elspeth. His letter continued,

> Here we are kept busy with work by cover of night. Earthworks, reinforced with timber, are being built. One of my jobs is to cut and carry the saplings to the men. Even though we work in darkness, the Rebs are not fooled, for they fire volleys of shell at us frequently. El, I wish you could see the big guns being moved into position. One hundred horses just to pull one gun! The horses are harnessed four across, and the teams are handled by dozens of men, all shouting and directing as the poor horses pull and strain to move the big Parrott guns through the mud. When the Rebs come up against these two hundred pound cannon shells, they will surely quit, and then the war will soon be finished. I will be so grateful to come home to a dry bed and dry clothes and dry food! Rain falls here almost daily, and I fear I will grow gills. Mosquitoes and fleas, however, do not seem to find the wet a hindrance, since we are plagued by the little rascals.

> I think of you often and carry your forget-me-not pouch with me. Please write soon. I remain faithfully yours.

> *Charles King*

Late in the afternoon of Saturday, May 3, the sky erupted with bursting shells coming from the Confederate breastworks. Charley found himself thrown to the ground as shot and shell exploded in the air and whizzed through the trees.

"Take cover! Take cover!" O'Toole shouted, but his voice was lost in the din of the explosions.

Realizing he was not wounded, but only stunned, Charley lifted himself and ran head down for cover behind a stack of wood. There he found Patrick, Frank, and Hans huddled with arms over their heads.

"What is it?" Hans mouthed.

"Enemy attack!" shouted Frank.

Throughout the intense bombardment, the men realized that, although shells flew in great number, they fell short of the camp and exploded in the tree tops or in the air. The fiery explosions continued into the night. Charley and the others watched trails of brilliant red light arc across the black sky in a magnificent display. Since communication was very difficult and movement restricted, there was little else to do but enjoy the spectacular entertainment.

Suddenly around midnight, the firing ceased. The smell of sulfur, the clouds of haze and smoke, and the blackness of night settled over all.

"It's an eerie feeling, so quiet," Charley whispered.

"Yeah, and no fires lit in camp," Patrick whispered back.

"Didn't need any. The Rebs provided light enough to read by. Now that it's quiet, I'm gonna get some sleep," Frank said as he walked toward his tent. "And why are you whispering?" he laughed.

Charley and Patrick grinned at each other. "I guess we just didn't want to spoil the quiet," Patrick said.

At first light the next morning, Charley was awakened by shouts. "The Rebs have gone! The Rebs have gone!" It had become apparent that the Confederates had used their massive bombardment to mask the retreat of their troops toward Williamsburg.

Now the Union troops were ecstatic as they moved into the trenches and earthworks so recently occupied by the Rebs. The boys of the drum corps were immediately organized and struck up the lively tunes which had so long been silenced during the stealthy work of the last month.

The Pennsylvania 49th marched into Yorktown to the tune of "Yankee Doodle." Every now and then Charley noticed a wooden stake with a rag fluttering at the top. A soldier stood guard at each of these, directing the columns of soldiers to take a wide path around them.

"Rebs sure left in a hurry," Charley shouted to Frank over the beat of his drum.

Frank nodded his head in agreement as they looked at the abandoned cannons still menacingly aimed at the woods where the 49th had been; the tents still standing row upon row, but slashed by knife or sword; the half-cooked meat doused with turpentine, hanging over cold cook fires; and the ground littered with piles of oyster shells, sardine boxes and empty bottles. The enemy made very sure not to provide comfort to the victorious Yanks.

Later, during a break in the music, Charley overheard talk of the "torpedoes" left randomly hidden by the Rebs to take the Yankees unaware.

"It's immoral, I say!" argued one older soldier indignantly. "Can't stand and fight like men are trained to, but have to ske-daddle and leave a hidden reminder just where one of ours is sitting down for a rest and a chance to quench his thirst!"

"What's he talking about?" Charley asked Jacob Adams.

"Apparently one man of the NY 36th sat down on a grassy knoll and found a pocketknife at his feet. Feelin' lucky, he reached down and saw a small cord wrapped 'round it. He gave it a jerk to break the cord, and in an instant, he was blown into smithereens, arms and legs flying, and what was left of him, burnt black. Others round him were injured, but not killed. One lost an eye, and another a leg!"

"Little Mac did right, by God! Making the Reb prisoners go ahead and dig them up first after that. Let the Rebs blow up their own if they want to play dirty, I say," said the indignant soldier.

"Right, boys," said Jacob Adams to all the drum corps. "You steer far clear of all those stakes topped with rags."

The 49th was not allowed much time for rest. The army trudged along Yorktown Road toward Williamsburg. "Keep a steady beat, lads, to give the men spirit," O'Toole encouraged the corps as they plowed through the mud in pursuit of the enemy. Charley thought it was hard to keep drumming and give the men spirit when they were standing still waiting behind bogged down horses and artillery.

"The Rebs have flooded the place," Frank said.

"Yeah, they release the floodgates on the dams after they pass through," muttered a soldier who stood knee deep in water.

"Sure plays havoc with moving men and wagons, to say nothing of the big guns," said another.

The sound of sporadic gunfire up ahead warned the troops of the looming battle. At dusk the rain began to fall once again. The men built crude shelters from tree branches or huddled under oilskins to bivouack for the night.

Charley, Frank, and Patrick built a rough lean-to in a muddy thicket. The three then ventured further into the woods to relieve themselves. Starting back to camp, they walked close to the edge of a small ravine to avoid the thick undergrowth on the floor of the woods.

Suddenly Frank grabbed both Charley and Patrick by the shoulders and pushed them down to the ground, whispering, "Shhhh! There's someone over there. I can hear them talkin' plain as day."

Huddled shoulder to shoulder on the slope of the ravine, the three boys listened, and sure enough, they heard another half-whispered conversation.

"I tell ya, I heard something directly 'cross that holler," a Southern voice said.

"Aw, that was just Jimmy peein' against the tree. Wasn't it, Jimmy?" There was a laugh, quickly hushed. Then another Southern drawl said, "You're always hearin' somethin'. Let's get on with it and open the flood gates so we can get back to camp afore we really do hear somethin'."

The footsteps retreated, but Charley, Frank, and Patrick remained silently lying on the muddy embankment, their hearts pounding. Charley felt himself slipping down the steep angle and dug the tips of his boots hard into the bank. The effort was futile. All three found themselves sliding downward in a sort of mudslide toward the stream bed.

They heard a sudden rush of approaching water, and frantically all three tried to scramble out of the knee-deep stream and up the muddy embankment. They grasped wildly at branches and small trees, but could not get footholds. A torrent of water from the opened floodgates crashed down upon them. Kicking and trying to keep their heads above water, they were swept downstream. Patrick was the first to see the fallen tree protruding from the bank. He was nearly beyond it by the time he reached out and clutched with one hand at a limb. With a jolt, Frank and Charley were washed against the tree trunk. Charley gripped the trunk with his free arm and clung to Frank's tunic with his other. He coughed from all the water he had swallowed and tried to shake it clear from his face so he could see what was going on. There was no protection from the branches and other objects sweeping into them.

The sound of a tree limb cracking was barely heard above the rushing water. "Help!" Patrick cried out as the branch supporting him gave way.

Frank, closest to Patrick, extended one arm out to him while holding tightly to the stronger end of the branch. "Take my hand! Take my hand!" he shouted.

Patrick reached desperately, brushing Frank's fingertips with his own. Thrusting his hand forward, Frank grasped Patrick's wrist tightly.

"Hold on!" Charley shouted, as he renewed his grip on the back of Frank's tunic and pulled with aching fingers as hard as he could against the weight of the two boys and the force of the current.

"No! Oh no!" Frank cried as Patrick was dragged free of his grasp. In seconds he was gone, hands and then boots flaying wildly in the water as he disappeared.

Frank's body went limp, and Charley struggled to support him. The force of the water on Frank's body nearly wrenched him away from Charley. "Don't give up, Frank, don't give up! Keep your head up!" he shouted. Then silently, "Please, God, not him too. Please, God." Charley pulled and pulled, closer to the bank and up against the exposed roots of the fallen tree. "Here. We can climb up here," he said.

Frank, dazed, finally followed Charley's directions as they dragged themselves clear of the water and then collapsed exhausted on the bank.

"He's gone, he's really gone! And it's all my fault," Frank said after the two were able to speak once more.

"It's not your fault, Frank. You did your best to help him. Maybe he'll be all right and climb out further downstream. He's got to be all right!"

"But I let him go! His hand slipped out of mine just like I let Meg's hand slip out of mine," Frank sobbed, his words barely understandable.

"What do you mean, Frank? Who is Meg?" Charley asked.

"Meg?" Frank said, his voice just a whisper. "Meg is my sister. We were running away from the orphan asylum. I jumped on a train. And I reached down for Meg. Her hand was in mine, but the train was moving, and she stumbled. And I let go . . . I let her go . . . I should have jumped back down, but I didn't. The train was going faster and faster. I saw her stand and brush off her dress. A buggy stopped beside her, and a woman got out. Then the train went around a bend, and that was the last I ever saw of her. And now Patrick is gone, too, all because of me." He groaned and stifled another sob.

Charley, still stunned by the loss of Patrick, didn't know what to say, but he let his hand rest on Frank's shoulder. Finally he broke the silence. "We've got to get back to camp, Frank. Maybe Sergeant O'Toole will send out a search party for Patrick."

"Not with the Rebs this close, he won't," Frank said in despair.

As the two boys, soaked and shivering, slowly made their way back to camp, Frank asked, "Why did you save me, Charley? You could have let me go and no one would be the wiser."

Charley searched his mind for an answer. "Because, I guess we're friends."

As soon as the two reached the bivouack site, O'Toole was upon them. "We thought the Rebs had ya for sure, lads. Where's Lynch?"

Charley and Frank reported what had occurred as well as they could. After listening, O'Toole, jaws clenched and eyes narrowed, said gruffly, "Get some hot coffee and some rest. Tomorrow we take Williamsburg." Then he turned away without further comment.

They looked at each other in surprise. "I thought he would at least try to find him," Charley said.

"Aw, Patrick is just another soldier to him," Frank said. "A cheap loss."

They fell into their lean-to exhausted and covered themselves as best they could against the drops of rain seeping through the rough structure. Just moments before sleep came to Charley, Frank reached out and touched his back.

"What is it?" Charley mumbled.

"Nothing. I just wanted to be sure," he said.

*   *   *

Frank lay there unable to sleep even though his body and limbs ached from the ordeal they had just been through. His mind raced with visions of Patrick being swept away from his grasp and then with visions of Meg's hand being pulled from his until the two visions became one and the same and all he could feel was despair and loss. But Charley . . . Charley, the little runt, had hung on to him like a bulldog. No one had ever cared about him or fought like that for him before. Well, Meg had cared. But Meg had been the little sister he had looked out for, and a lot of good he had been to her in the long run . . . And how was she surviving now? "I'll find you, Meg. I promise I'll find you." He stared into the night.

Later, Frank saw a silhouette in the darkness bend above him and Charley. He closed his eyes and pretended sleep as Sergeant O'Toole placed an oilskin over them. He watched through half-closed eyes as the sergeant quietly gathered up Patrick's personal effects to be sent home.

*　　*　　*

Chapter Nine

Battle of Williamsburg —— May 5, 1862

Click, click, click. Charley was awakened by the sound. It grew louder, diminishing the drumming of the rain lashing against the lean-to. At first he thought he was at home in the warm, dry featherbed, but that thought was only momentary as the reality of the wet and chill penetrated his body. Stumbling into the darkness and peering through the curtain of rain, he saw groups of men gathered under what shelter they could find, snapping the caps of their guns in order to dry the gun barrels. Click, click, click. As he walked to the edge of the woods, the sound followed him and grew louder as the sleepless men prepared themselves for battle. Charley stared into the dismal woods and hoped against hope that Patrick would appear.

As the black sky changed to gray, men huddled in the wet and boiled coffee over smoky campfires where they could. The sound of clicking rifles grew to a crescendo like huge locusts devouring a grassy field. Here and there Charley could see men sewing bits of cloth into the collars of their jackets.

The boys of the drum corps huddled together to listen as Sergeant O'Toole explained last minute preparations for battle.

"Why are the men sewing their jackets, Sergeant?" asked Charley.

O'Toole straightened up to his full height, pulled his cap lower over his eyes, "That's in case of wounds, or worse, lads, so the family can be notified, ya know." His voice trailed off and lowered toward the end of his reply, so the boys needed to strain to hear.

"Should we do that, Sergeant?"

"No need, no need, lads. Yer job is to stand out of harm's way, and with a steady beat direct our brave, fight'n men back to our unit. We'll be sendin' no notifications to yer families . . . with the help of God."

"But Sergeant, what if . . .?" Hans did not finish the question.

"If it makes ya feel better, laddie, put yer name in yer boot," O'Toole bellowed, eager to move on to other subjects. "Soon we'll be on the march, no time for cookfires or mess tents. Yer rations will have to last till this battle's done, if it's one hour or one week. So listen careful now."

The boys leaned in closer to hear.

"If ya have the opportunity to acquire food for yerselves, do it. No matter if it's from a dead comrade or enemy, do it. Don't worry about blankets or haversacks or anything else. Food is what will keep ya goin' and food is what ya will need. Yer not home at Mama's kitchen table now, lads, so don't be squeamish."

They hardly had time to absorb this new information when a burst of cannon and gunfire, not too distant, shook the ground beneath them. The sudden interruption ceased the talk and the incessant clicking. All eyes turned in the direction of the sound. Sergeant O'Toole pulled his watch from his pocket.

"It's just gone half past seven. It's begun."

All morning Charley, Frank, and Hans listened to the rumble and roar of battle, expecting at any moment to be ordered into the thick of it. But, as Jacob Adams said, they were a part of General

"Baldy" Smith's division, and someone must have other plans for them. Countless times Charley reread his most recent letter from home and checked his most prized possessions—Grandpa Eb's knife deep in his pants pocket and the leather forget-me-not pouch with the lock of Elspeth's golden hair in his breast pocket.

Finally around noon, the Pennsylvania 49th, as part of General Winfield Hancock's brigade, was ordered to move. With three days' rations in their haversacks, a drenching rain falling, ankle deep mud underfoot, and drums silent, the huge body of men moved snakelike across creek and flooded fields. The noise of thousands of boots pulling against the tugging mud was the only sound to be heard.

They seemed to be taking a wide path to the right, away from the action, and at one point Charley glimpsed an expanse of the York River. Then, before he knew it, they crossed an old mill bridge and, without gunfire, took possession of an abandoned Confederate redoubt. Holding Old Betsy protectively to his side and balancing by digging his heels into the muddy bank of the earthworks, Charley half walked, half slid down into the long, wide trenched redoubt. They were given no time to settle in.

"Move out, men. We're taking up position at the next redoubt. Follow me!" Captain Sweeney ordered, and Charley, with the rest of the company, struggled up the muddy embankment.

"Ha, them Rebs are so busy with old man Sumner and his boys, they don't even know we're here," said one grizzled old soldier, spitting tobacco juice.

"Silence in the ranks," growled O'Toole in a low and menacing voice.

In their new position, an expanse of open plain, with two more occupied Confederate redoubts, spread between them and the ongoing battle at Fort Magruder. The mist of rain and low-lying gunsmoke obscured their view, but flashes of cannon fire could be seen. Mired in mud, horses and men strained to place artillery pieces into position.

Captain Sweeney moved among the troops. "Keep your powder dry, men. The same rain is falling on Johnny Reb. Just make sure your gunpowder is dry."

"Must be coming soon," Frank said. "Officers are getting nervous." He motioned with his head toward Captain Sweeney.

The shouted command of "Ready, Aim, Fire!" was given, and the sound of field cannon boomed through the air. Charley covered his ears as the ground vibrated beneath his feet. Again and again the Federal artillery pounded shell from their position into the nearby enemy redoubts. Between bursts of cannon, skirmishers aimed rifle shots at the Confederate troops. Those who could escape did and retreated toward Fort Magruder and Williamsburg. Those less fortunate lay sprawled halfway out of the redoubt or on the flat, muddy plain.

"Wonder why we ain't movin' up closer and takin' over?" Hans said to Charley and Frank. Sitting on the slope of the redoubt, oilskins placed over the mud in a vain effort to protect themselves from the wet, the boys chewed on hardtack.

"Don't worry, lads, we'll be seeing more action soon enough," O'Toole answered Hans' question. "The general's probably just waitin' on reinforcements. Then we'll see fightin' galore."

For three long hours, intermittent skirmishes continued with no reinforcements in sight. Frustration among the troops and officers was growing. O'Toole sloshed through ankle-deep water back and forth, consulting his pocket watch every few minutes.

"Sergeant, aren't we ever going to do anything?" Charley asked.

O'Toole turned to Charley with fury on his face. "Are ya callin' us cowardly, lad?" But when he saw Charley's innocent look, he realized the question was an honest one. "Ya'll wait and do as yer ordered. So pull up yer boots and shut yer gobs till yer told to move. And don't ask so many questions!" Turning his broad back, O'Toole pounded through the muddy water away from the boys of the drum corps.

Jacob Adams was sitting near. "Don't worry, boys, you just ruffled his feathers a bit. You know, war is not all glory and parades. War is waiting and picking at the enemy like a mosquito, nip here, nip there, wait and wait, and when the time comes, the final big bite. That's what we are doing now. Nipping, nipping, and waiting. To be a soldier, you have to have ten percent courage and ninety percent patience."

A sudden flurry of activity on the plain drew everyone's attention and officers began shouting orders.

The boys jumped to their feet and readied their drums, but almost immediately they, along with the entire infantry, were ordered to lie flat on the ground just behind the crest of a small ridge.

Silently they watched a whole brigade of gray move toward them, led by an old general hunched in his saddle and waving his sword. As the Confederates moved closer and closer, Charley's heart pounded harder, and he and Frank looked wordlessly into each other's eyes. A deep-voiced rumble of hundreds of men began, and gradually they could make out the words "Bull Run! Ball's Bluff! Bull Run! Ball's Bluff!" repeated over and over in a mocking chant. The mass moved laboriously but steadily through the sodden, muddy plain toward the Union troops as they lay hidden in wait. It seemed endless and at the same time momentary.

When the chant grew louder and louder and the enemy was nearly upon them, General Hancock, mounted on his horse, appeared. Hatless and waving his sword in the air, he galloped above the line of troops and shouted orders in his hoarse voice, "Forward! Charge!"

With a roar of cheers the Federal troops stood, advanced over the crest of the ridge and shot directly into the ranks of the surprised enemy. Captain Sweeney ordered, "Drummers, sound the long roll and keep it going during attack!" Charley took his position behind the regimental flag. He beat his drum and did not falter. He did not look down, but kept his eyes on the Pennsylvania

49th regimental flag directly in front of him. He played his drum hard and loud; his arms were numb as he continued beating out a rallying point to the men of his company.

Through the smoke he could see the Rebel force disintegrate. Many waved white handkerchiefs in surrender. The dead and wounded lay on the field, and yet the Federal troops continued to advance. Finally a cease-fire order came. The gunfire stopped, but the moaning of the wounded did not.

"Drummers, assemble the regiment!" O'Toole shouted, and Charley changed his drum cadence. Through the dispersing smoke Charley saw Frank moving slowly, head down, beating a slow march.

Amidst the chaos a Federal cavalry officer reached down from his mount, seized a Confederate battle flag, and with a great triumphant yell waved it above his head for all to see. Cheers from the victorious Yankees rose up all around, and Charley joined in, as Lieutenant Custer galloped up and down before the exultant Yankees and defeated Rebel prisoners, displaying the captured colors.

Charley, filled with pride, turned to join the others. He tripped and fell, sprawling across something soft. Turning his head, Charley looked into the staring eyes of a dead Confederate soldier. Horrified, Charley recoiled and pulled himself up to his feet. He could not take his eyes away. A rifle with fixed bayonet lay next to the body. The dead man's hands covered his stomach as though he were trying to push back into place the intestines which oozed through his spread fingers and on to the ground in a bloody gray mass. Charley looked down at his own hands, now red from the dead man's blood. He reached down to try to wipe them clean across the Rebel's trousers. Then he vomited. He retched until he felt empty. Staggering back to join his unit, Charley stood white faced and mute, awaiting further orders. When they came, the duty was not pleasant.

"Lift his head. I'll take the legs," Frank said to Charley as they worked along with others, moving the wounded back to the field hospitals.

"This is a Reb. Shouldn't we take our own first?" Charley asked.

"Well, this fellow's not hurt too bad, just bleeding from the shoulder, but bleeding pretty fast. If we can get him to the Doc, maybe he can save him."

"I sure hope there's some Rebs who think like you, and will help Patrick."

Frank nodded his head sadly. Thinking of their lost friend, they lifted the slight figure and headed for the yellow flag identifying the barn as a field hospital for Confederate prisoners. The prisoner moved and suddenly kicked and twisted as the boys struggled to keep their balance. Placing the Reb on the ground, Frank reached down to open the top buttons of the gray tunic.

"Keep your dirty Yankee hands off me!" the Reb said as he clutched his tunic to his chest and sat up.

"Simmer down, mister. We're just tryin' to help you breathe better."

The Reb, eyes wide and still clutching at the front of his tunic, looked from one face to the other. Then looking at Frank, said, "I'm no mister. I'm Charlotte Langford of Langford Plantation, Virginia."

"A girl!" exclaimed Charley. "You can't be much older than we are!"

"I'm sixteen years old and I joined up to fight like my papa and brothers," she replied. "You'd be surprised how many of us women make it into the war, disguised as men."

"You won't get much older than sixteen either if you don't let us get you to the surgery to stop that bleeding," said Frank.

"What for? They'll shoot me anyway."

"No, probably just send you home to your ma, since you're a girl."

At this, her hazel eyes flared, "Home, home, you say. What home? After you pirating, sneaking Yankees finished with it, there was nothing left. The last thing I saw as I rode away with my mama and little sisters was Grandma's grand piano out on the lawn with the lid lifted and the inside filled with hay for the dratted Yankee officers' horses to feed from." Gasping for breath, her voice weaker, she continued, "Ignorant pigs, all of them. That's why I'm fighting. If I'm to be shot, then so be it. I'll be proud to die for . . ." The last words unspoken, Charlotte Langford fainted.

"Charley, you go ahead to tell the surgery that a wounded Confederate woman is being brought in," said Frank.

*   *   *

Then he bent and slid an arm under her shoulders and the other beneath her knees, gently lifting her. Her head rested against his shoulder. Dark curly hair, cropped short, brushed against his cheek. Her blood soaked his uniform. Her hair is so soft, Frank thought. For all of her tough soldier talk, she's just a little thing, like a wounded bird. A feeling of tenderness swept over him. He hoped that he would not be too late to save this brave young woman.

Countless trips later, Frank, drooping from exhaustion, found himself alone back at the yellow flag. "Let's see how Miss Charlotte Langford is abiding," Frank told himself in a poor mimic of a Southern drawl.

He found her lying freshly bandaged on a pile of straw in a corner apart from the other prisoner patients. She eyed him defiantly in silence. But before he could speak she said, "You Yankees have won nothing. Do not be in a hurry to shout victory. We kept you in Yorktown for an entire month building your fancy defenses. Then we gave you Yorktown as a gift when it was no longer of use to us. You may have caught up with us in Williamsburg, but Richmond is still a long way off. Just you wait till you hit those Chickahominy marshes in the summer heat. The swamp fever will do more to destroy your forces than all the cannons and battle works you'll face before Richmond."

Awed by the anger and hate directed at him by this wounded girl propped on her bed of straw, Frank felt wounded himself by her sharp tongue. He shoved his hands deeply into his pockets and replied, "Well, that may be, miss, but I just stopped by to see how you were gettin' on."

She stared at him, her eyes briefly liquid with tears, and then with an upward jerk of her chin, she looked away at the coarse wall of the barn. There was nothing he could say or do, but he knew that he would not forget Miss Charlotte Langford.

*   *   *

Chapter Ten

The Town of Williamsburg, Virginia —— May 6, 1862

The first light of May 6 streaked the sky pink and held promise of warmth and sunshine. The battlefield, littered with the
dead and pockmarked by cannon shell, was left behind as the
Pennsylvania 49th marched into the town of Williamsburg. The
orchards laden with blossoms and the blooming dogwoods, daf-
fodils, and violets could not help but lift the spirits of the men.

Union troops swarmed over the town occupying any available
open spaces. Tents sprang up in the center green and lawns. Red
flags appeared on buildings of the College of William and Mary
to indicate hospitals for the Union wounded. And confiscated
homes were used for officer headquarters. Many of the townspeople had fled to Richmond leaving slaves and old folks to the
mercy of the occupying army. Picket fences were torn down and
used as firewood by the Yankees, and livestock were confiscated
to feed the thousands of men who had been living on hardtack
and salt pork for several days.

Charley looked at the busy sights around him. Men on horses,
all moving quickly by; units marching; wounded on stretchers
being carried to hospitals; horses whinnying; wagons rumbling;

orders being shouted. But above it all boomed out the voice of O'Toole, "LYNCH!"

Charley jumped to his feet. Marching down the center of the cobbled street was a mismatched group of Union soldiers escorted by mounted cavalry, and right in front with a big grin on his face, marched Patrick Lynch! Charley ran forward.

"Company halt!" commanded the officer. "Men, report to your company headquarters." And with that, the happy former prisoners dispersed. Patrick was soon surrounded by the boys of the corps, all talking, shouting, back slapping, and handshaking at once.

O'Toole shouted, "Stand off! Give the man a chance! Lynch, over there is our bivouac. Get yourself settled. Then report to me. The rest of ya, if ya have not duties, I'll be happy to oblige."

The boys scattered back to duties less stringent than O'Toole's threatened assignments. Charley and Frank hung back.

"All right, all right, lads. See Lynch get settled in," he said as he strode away toward regimental headquarters.

Immediately Patrick was again inundated with questions from Charley and Frank as they walked toward the bivouac site. "What happened, Patrick? We thought you drowned!" "Who pulled you out or did you pull yourself out?"

Finally in what privacy the three could find inside the small tent, Patrick told his story.

"I washed up against another tree farther down the creek, and I just clung there till the water went down. I even slept, too tired to move, even to pull myself out of the water. When I opened my eyes, there was two Rebs laughin' at me, 'Well, well, lookie here at this funny lookin' fish we caught.' They pulled me out and wrapped up my head where I clunked myself on a rock, I suppose, rubbed me down with a blanket, and gave me some hot coffee to warm my insides. I was shivrin' so hard, I couldn't stop shakin' for an hour. Then they walked me to their camp. By this time the battle was ragin'. I could hear it all around, and I thought about you. I just sat there in their camp on the wrong side of the guns, and little by little other prisoners were brought in.

"Then early this morning we were on the road again. The Reb guards were just a ragtag band with a lieutenant in charge—not many more of them than us, but they had the guns and horses. There was one fellow who was a 'long drink of water,' name of Malcolm. He got off his horse to let a wounded Yank ride, and he gave me some of his hardtack to eat.

"Well, pretty soon, we all heard the pounding of horses' hooves comin' on fast. The lieutenant calls, 'Riflemen to the rear with me. Enemy cavalry approachin'.' Then he says, 'Prisoners, quick, double time.' And we just all looked at each other and stopped dead in our tracks. 'Prisoners, move quick or we will shoot!' he shouts again, gettin' more nervous by the minute. So we sit right down in the road. Now, our boys is in sight, see, so we all start cheerin'. 'Stand and fight!' shouts the lieutenant. I guess he forgot to shoot us. Anyway, Malcolm . . ."

"The long drink of water?" Frank broke in.

"Yeah," replied Patrick. "Anyway, he takes a position behind a split rail fence. Our boys come ridin' up on the group, shootin' away. We all crouch down low and when I look up, it was all over. Then we formed up to march back to our lines, this time with some prisoners of our own. I saw Malcolm slumped across the split rail fence, so long and skinny that he touched ground on both sides. He won't share his horse or hardtack no more." Patrick looked down at the ground. "I felt kinda bad about that."

Both Frank and Charley were quiet with their own thoughts, until Frank spoke, "I know what you mean, Pat. These Rebs—they're not so different than us."

Charley was sure Frank was thinking of Miss Charlotte Langford.

Late in the day Charley found some time to himself to write two letters. The first one to his family was shorter because suddenly he could not bear to tell his family of the horrors of battle and the grim conditions he had just lived through. He let them know that he was well and safe and that he had just demolished a delicious bowl of chicken stew fresh from the yards of Williamsburg and sweet potato baked on the coals of the fire.

The second letter to Elspeth was different.

Williamsburg, Virginia
May 6, 1862

My Dear Elspeth,

We have been through a terrible battle and a grimmer day I cannot imagine. Frank and I spent long hours carrying the wounded and dead from the battlefield. El, I cannot begin to put into words the sounds and smells and sights of war. We found two men—one in blue and one in gray lying face to face—each stabbed through with the other's bayonette. You would not wish to be a drummer boy now. However, you will be interested to hear that one of the wounded Rebels Frank and I removed to the hospital turned out to be a girl with hair cut off, in uniform, and as feisty as any fighting man.

We thought we had lost Patrick in a gully wash, but he was captured by the enemy and then freed by our boys, so we are all together still, excepting for you of course.

Sutlers have swarmed into all our camps to sell their wares, but they are not honest men like your father. One greedy man actually charged five dollars for a dozen eggs! We joke that these merchants should have the guns since they rob us regularly. Frank and I took revenge on one profiteer today. I pretended to be interested in buying some needles and thread at the front of the wagon, while Frank crept up to the rear and "borrowed" the biggest sweet potato you ever saw. He stuffed it under his tunic, and we strolled away as calm as you please. We roasted it in the hot ashes of the fire and had a wonderful meal, all four of us.

El, you would love Williamsburg now that the battle is over. Trees and flowers are in bloom here. It would be a fine place for us to walk and talk as we did back in Lewinsville. I guess you are my best friend. General McClellan is leading us on to Richmond and once we have taken that city as we have taken Williamsburg, I am sure this war will be over.

Until then, I remain faithfully yours,
Charles King

The civilized atmosphere and relative luxury of Williamsburg was short-lived. Within two days the Pennsylvania 49th was in pursuit of the Confederate forces and headed toward the dreaded marshes of the Chickahominy River.

Chapter Eleven

The Chickahominy River, Virginia —— May–June, 1862

Charley and Frank trudged along the road, their drums bouncing idly against their sides. At some point with the never-ending heat, rain, and mud, formation and marching had been abandoned, and everyone seemed to travel at his own pace. Some stragglers didn't even catch up to their regiments at night and just pitched tents where they could find a spot out of the sticky, yellow mud. O'Toole, however, kept an eagle eye on the drum corps, to be sure they stayed together.

Charley tried to ignore the hunger pains which gnawed at his stomach. His mind kept wandering back to the mouthwatering chicken stew and roasted sweet potato they had feasted on in Williamsburg. The supply wagons, they were told, were mired in the mud just outside Williamsburg, and the men marched on with what little rations they had with them. Twice they passed well-tended plantations which flew the white flag of protection. Little Mac had ordered that no Confederates who had remained on their land be molested. Provost marshals were posted at the houses and other strategic points to insure the protection of the occupants and properties. Women in long calico dresses, some holding babies, with Negroes clustered around, stood silently on their porches as the "Yankees" marched past.

The hungry troops looked longingly at the crops and farm animals and grumbled among themselves. "Plenty o' drinkin' water in that well," and, "Sure could make a nice fire with that ol' fence post."

"Yeah, good enough to cook up that sweet little piglet, yonder," came the reply.

But the troops passed on—ladies of the plantation and hungry fighting men silently contemplating each other.

Up at dawn to sound reveille, the drum corps and troops of the Pennsylvania 49th proceeded a mile or two and then pulled up to rest through the worst heat of the day. The sun was out, and steam rose from the wet wool of their uniforms which were spread out to dry. The last of the hardtack had been eaten, and murky swamp water was the only liquid in sight. Some slept from exhaustion, others just took what rest they could. Charley lay in the shade of a pine tree, his eyes closed, daydreaming of Elspeth offering him a cool drink of water from a long handled gourd.

"All right, lads," said O'Toole to the boys. "It looks as though our supply wagons are sunk in this yellow wax they call mud hereabouts, so we'll have ta do for ourselves if we want ta eat between now and whenever it is that they dig them out. Remember our orders are ta treat the people here with respect. If ya see the white flag, that means one of our own, God help us, will arrest ya for stealin' without a second thought. Ya'll be takin' nothin' that ya'll not be payin' for. Ya'll take nothin' without permission, not even a drink a' water to wet your whistle. However, should ya find a place abandoned, that means the folks deserted to the Rebel lines. And that means they are true 'Secess' and all's fair ta take."

Hans, Patrick, Charley, and Frank found a rutted lane which ran through the tall pine trees. The lane ended in an overgrown, grassy farmyard with a sagging barn and a weathered frame house. No white flag flew, no guards were posted.

"Maybe it's abandoned, and I see a rooster," Hans shouted over his shoulder as he bolted to the farmyard in pursuit.

Soon all four boys were running, shouting, and waving their arms in the air as the rooster, feathers ruffled, darted just out of reach.

"Hey, you younguns, what are you doin' to my old banty-rooster?" An old woman stuck her head out a window to shout at them.

All four boys froze in their tracks, surprised by the unexpected voice. "We ain't stealin', ma'am. We can pay you fifty cents for it," replied Hans.

"Hmmm," an old gnarled hand rubbed across a wrinkled face. "How'll I get up a mornin' without my old cock-a-crow?"

Charley could almost taste the delicious chicken stew. He licked his lips and said, "Would one dollar help you to decide, ma'am?"

The head disappeared from the window and within a few seconds, the door was flung wide open. "Come in, young gentlemen, come in."

After further negotiations, the woman offered to cook the rooster for an additional twenty-five cents. Somehow, while that process took place, the boys found themselves doing small chores around the farm. "My old legs ain't what they used to be. If you'd just split some of that wood yonder," she said to Frank. "And stack it on the porch outside the door, I'll have enough to keep this here fire goin'."

With growling stomachs, the other three boys pulled weeds and mended a hole in the fence, urged on by the tantalizing smell of the simmering "old cock" on the stove.

At last the stew was ready. The weary boys were invited to sit at the kitchen table. They devoured the stew, biscuits, and fresh buttermilk, while the old woman sat in a rocker, contentedly smoking a clay pipe.

"I'll allow as how you Lincolnite Yankees ain't as bad as I'd supposed," she said.

The boys arrived back at camp at dusk—Charley cradling his cap full of fresh eggs. Frank and Patrick each carried leftover biscuits and a sack of flour. Hans had an armful of last year's apples from the old lady's cold cellar bundled in his jacket. Sergeant O'Toole added their items to the company's newly acquired cache of food.

In the two weeks after the battle of Williamsburg, the Pennsylvania 49th along with all the Federal soldiers marched only a frustrating, wearying forty miles. The conditions of rain, mud, or blazing heat which dried the thick mud into layers of penetrating dust began to take its toll on the men. Charley and Frank watched some of the older men grow sick, whether from the heat, the drinking water, or the constantly biting mosquitoes, they did not know. The swamp fever became more and more common as the columns proceeded deeper into the swampy areas surrounding the Chickahominy River.

Bivouacked near a crossroads one evening, the boys saw a signpost with an arrow pointed west and marked "Richmond 20 miles."

"Only 20 miles! We should take Richmond soon," Charley exclaimed.

"We will, laddie, in due time. It's 20 mile as the crow flies, but not as an army marches. We are to follow this meandering river, up to Richmond. Round and about, I agree, but the best path," replied Sergeant O'Toole.

"I sure hope our mail catches up with us soon," said Patrick. "Philadelphia is a lot more than 20 miles away, and in the other direction."

"How far are we from home?" asked Hans.

Jacob Adams thought a moment and said, "I reckon about 300 miles from old Philly."

Patrick rubbed his chin. "Blazes, that's a long, long way from there to here." That night Charley noticed that Patrick sat by the fire after the others had gone to sleep.

The next morning as the men left the crossroads they laughed to see a new arrow nailed under the one to Richmond. This arrow pointed due north and read "Filladelfia 326 miles."

The daily marching finally came to an end when the Pennsylvania 49th was posted along the Chickahominy for picket duty. The boys were kept busy raising platforms to lift their beds above the marshy ground. They built lean-tos with tree boughs placed on top to ward off the one hundred degree temperatures, but this gave little protection from the humid, scorching heat. Warned not to drink the swampy water, some of the soldiers, desperate with thirst, found themselves straining water through cloth to "purify" it. More and more red flags appeared in front of hospital tents as swamp fever ran rampant through the camp.

"Wagons a comin'!" The word spread quickly. Charley and the others gathered in groups, watching for the first of the wagons to appear on the furrowed road that led into camp.

"Sure hope they got us some decent drinking water," said Frank. "I'd give anything for a cool drink of clear water."

"Yeah, and mosquito nettin' too, so we can sleep some without bein' bit to death. Why, I heard tell that the other night three of them critters got on a pack mule, one on each ear and one on the tail, and they carried him clean away," laughed Patrick.

The wagons rolled into camp. Weary drivers and mules caked in mud were evidence of how difficult the journey had been. By that evening the supplies were distributed. The aroma of coffee brewing and food cooking lifted the spirits of the men. Despite the heat and humidity, they all looked forward to a hot meal and, most of all, to coffee.

"Adams, King, Lynch, Schmidt," O'Toole called the names and handed out long delayed packets of letters. Most of the drum corps received something. All laughed as Hans opened a parcel from home and pulled out a pair of gloves.

"My ma heard it gets cool at night around here. I'll really need these." Even Frank joined in the laughter, although he was the only one who received nothing.

"I expect he's used to it by now," Patrick said in a low voice to Charley.

"Don't know if you can ever get used to it," Charley replied as he watched Frank walk away from the excited crowd.

Toward evening, Charley and Frank came across Jacob Adams with his tall frame bowed against a tree. His face was covered by his hands, but his long beard quivered, and the muscles of his bare arms were tensed and strained. The boys were hesitant to approach this man who was always so in control and knowledgeable about so many things. They backed off, instinctively realizing his need for privacy.

"Maybe it's the swamp fever," Charley whispered to Frank.

Frank shook his head. "It's not fever that's got him," he whispered in return. "This is something else. Most likely news from home."

"We'd better tell Sergeant O'Toole," Charley said.

The boys watched as O'Toole approached Jacob who had not moved. He put a hand on his shoulder and said, "What is it, man?"

Jacob half turned, then handed him a letter, crumpled and damp from the sweat of his hands. "Three months past," he said. "Three months and I did not know." Then, in control and very simply he spoke, "It's from a neighbor. My wife and little girl died from the influenza. And my son, Robby, all alone, joined up to look for me. He's just sixteen, Michael, only a boy. I must find him."

"Yes, Jacob, yes. We will find him," O'Toole answered. He stood in silence, and then finally pressing his hand on Jacob's shoulder again, he and the boys walked away.

Much later, in the heavy closeness of the night. Charley and Frank heard the mournful strains of Jacob's fiddle. A beautiful melody drifted from the trees just beyond camp. The men listened and even the animals stirred. From somewhere in the darkness a tenor voice put words to the melody "Beautiful dreamer, awake unto me . . ."

When the music stopped, the notes hung on the humid air. Then came a Southern voice out of the wilderness, distant yet close enough to be heard by all, "That was nice, Yank. Give us another."

The camp along the Chickahominy grew as new troops arrived daily. Each day Charley and Frank watched Jacob Adams walk along the ranks of marching men who passed through. He would hold his hand about shoulder high, then point to his own hair. Even though he could not be heard, the men of his regiment knew the question Jacob asked. "He is about so tall, young he is, just sixteen; hair rusty red color, goes by the name of Robby Adams." Each time the soldiers shook their heads no. Sometimes one or two would reply, "Sorry, mister, don't know any youngin' like that" or just "Sorry, no."

A few weeks later Charley, Frank, and Hans were practicing drum rolls as Patrick played a lively tune on his fife. A ragtag group of abandoned slaves arrived at camp looking for food. A small Negro boy of about ten wandered from the group and approached the drummers. Fascinated by the music, he stood transfixed. Then slowly he began to dance. His bare feet lightly tapped the ground as his small hands clapped in rhythm to the drum beat. Soon the other men gathered around in a circle to watch.

When the tune finished, the crowd of men disbursed to reveal the small boy, breathing heavily and smiling brightly.

"What's your name?" asked Patrick.

"Joseph my name, mister."

"Hello, Joe, nice to meet you."

The boy did not respond to Patrick, but silently stared at Charley.

"What is it, Joseph?" Charley asked.

The boy pointed his index finger at Charley's drum.

"Oh, that's Old Betsy," Charley said. "Do you want to try it?"

Unbelieving, Joseph nodded. Charley lifted the strap of Old Betsy over the boy's head where it hung loosely from the small shoulders. Standing behind him, Charley placed the drumsticks in Joseph's hands, and with his own hands on top, he began to beat out a slow rhythm. Joseph's eyes brightened as he played.

Patrick began a tune on the fife, and the other drummers joined in. Soon Charley stepped back as Joseph continued to beat the drum and walk around in a small circle, smiling happily.

"Come away now, Joseph, and stop bothering the young gentlemen," said a deep voice. Joseph stopped and turned toward the tall, bearded black man who spoke. The music of the fife and drums stopped, and all eyes stared at the commanding presence. "Give back the drum now, and thank the gentlemen."

In one movement Joseph removed the drum strap and carried Old Betsy to Charley. With sad eyes he said, "Thank you, mister," and handed Charley the drum.

The large man extended his arm, engulfing Joseph's small hand in his own. He nodded, and as the boys of the drum corps watched, Joseph was led away.

By mid-June, with the ranks of the sick growing each day, General McClellan issued an order that every officer and soldier of the army be given half a gill of whiskey daily. Charley stood in line awaiting his turn and watched as some of the men drank down the burning liquid in one gulp before leaving the area. Others held their cups close and went to find a seat, sipping theirs little by little to savor the taste.

"Hey, I just saw you a minute ago. Back for another?" joked one corporal to a fellow soldier.

"Sure wish I could come through twice. This little bit ain't enough to keep a flea happy."

"Well, Little Mac says it will keep you from gettin' sick."

"Ya mean if I get sick, I'll get more? Sure do feel a cough comin' on. Why, it might even be pneumonia," laughed the second man.

All the while Chaplain Rutherford paced the length of the line, ranting on about this un-Christian behavior. "Better to suffer an ignominious defeat than to issue such an order!" he bellowed. "Think of the anguish this will bring to your mothers, wives, and sisters!"

As the boys of the drum corps approached their turns, Chaplain Rutherford spoke directly to them. "Satan will take control of you, young men! Do not lower your morals!"

At that Sergeant O'Toole approached the expounding preacher. "Now, now, Chaplain," he said as he placed his arm around the stiff shoulders of the indignant man. "Ya don't want ta be puttin' the fear of the divil inta the lads. Sure, a wee drop never did anyone any harm. It's only preventin' against the fever. Isn't it the orders from on high we're obeyin'?"

"It's the morality of the order I am questioning, Sergeant!" Chaplain Rutherford could still be heard arguing as Sergeant O'Toole led him away from the ranks.

"Did you ever have any whiskey?" Charley asked.

"Tasted some punch with whiskey in once," Hans replied. "Kind of warm feeling."

Patrick said, "My pa let me have some one time when we were fishin' and it got real cold and rainy. Trick is to sip it and not drink it too fast."

Since Patrick was the experienced one on the subject, the boys pushed him ahead of them in line so they could follow his expert example. Charley, Frank, and Hans watched Patrick as he lifted the cup to his lips.

"Aw, nothin' to it," he bragged as he threw his head back and tossed the whiskey down his throat as he had seen the soldiers do. He immediately started to cough and sputter. Dropping the empty tin cup to the ground, he grasped his throat with both hands, as his eyes filled with tears and his face turned crimson. "Water, water," he managed to squeak.

Charley quickly offered his canteen to Patrick, who gratefully began to drink.

"Ah, a good demonstration of what not to do," laughed Hans.

Charley looked at Patrick's red face and then down at the small amount of amber liquid in his cup. He turned the cup over and watched the thin stream sink into the ground. "I think the reverend is right," he said.

Hans looked at Charley. "Me, too." And he tipped his cup, pouring out its contents.

"Well, if you'd just sip and not be a pig, it's all right," said Frank as he took a sip of his ration.

"Aw . . . it just went down the wrong pipe," said Patrick.

"Sure, sure," said Hans, and they all laughed. Even Patrick had to laugh at his own bravado.

Chapter Twelve

The Seven Days Battle —— June, 1862

As the end of June and impending battle approached, tensions mounted.

"The Rebs sure are getting closer to us. Our pickets can hear the Rebs shoutin' orders, and they say there must be thousands of 'em just over yonder on the same side of the river we're on," Patrick said.

"Funny thing, though," said Frank. "The pickets told me they hear the orders, but they don't hear the heavy tramp of men. They must tread awful light, s'all I can say. And I don't like the feelin' of Johnny Reb breathin' down my back without even a river between us."

"Looks like only a small stand of woods and maybe a farm field separatin' us," said Hans.

"But look at it this way," said Charley. "We could be with the first Union troops to march into Richmond."

On the 25th of June a rumble of cannon and artillery fire erupted to the south of them in a place called Oak Grove. Sergeant O'Toole spoke to the corps throughout the day, reminding them of "duty, honor, and country" as he put it. Going over the commands, he reminded the boys that "thirty paces to the rear is your order. Stand firm and play through smoke and haze to give our boys heart and direction."

"A big one's coming soon, or mother hen O'Toole would not be fluttering around so much," Frank said to Charley.

The following day, June 26, battle broke out several miles to the north of them on the other side of the Chickahominy. A smoky haze drifted toward them accompanied by a background of more distant artillery fire. The boys paced the camp nervously, unsure about when they would be called into battle and from what direction it would come. Were the Union troops attacking or were the Rebs? They checked and rechecked their three days' food ration and their haversacks. Charley hastily scribbled short notes to Elspeth and his family and deposited them safely at the mail wagon. By afternoon a sporadic stream of wounded Union troops, some walking, some piled into wagons, arrived at the hospital tents. Rumors of General Porter's troops trying to hold back A. P. Hill's Confederates at Mechanicsville spread quickly.

Next morning cannon fire shook the boys awake. "Holy jumpin' Jehosaphat, where's that comin' from?" Patrick shouted as he pulled on his boots. They had no time to wonder about their situation.

"Sound assembly!" O'Toole shouted.

Captain Sweeney addressed Company F. "Our orders are to defend against the enemy on this side of the river. General Porter is presently engaging the enemy across the Chickahominy. We will be ready should they come from the Richmond lines. Strike camp. We take up defense positions within the hour. God bless you all."

The troops moved from camp, swatting at the ever-present mosquitoes and grumbling about the already intense heat. The rumble of battle to the north continued in the background. The Pennsylvania 49th, as part of General Winfield Hancock's Brigade, was deployed at a small farm not far from the camp.

Pickets were placed around the perimeter. The men rested where they could, some leaning on fence posts or walls, others stretched out in the shade of the porches or in the cooler shelter of the barn. All kept their weapons within easy reach and all tried to store up their energy for the battle certain to come.

"Do you think we could maybe find an egg or two in that chicken coop?" asked Patrick hopefully as the boys sat under a willow tree. It was long past noon, but Patrick was the only one chewing on a piece of hardtack.

"Naw," said Hans. "Won't even find a feather left in there. This family is long gone over yonder." He nodded his head in the general direction of Richmond. "And took everything that could move with them, . . . pure Secess."

"Yeah, and you better save that hardtack because we don't know how long we'll be here if those Rebs come pouring out of Richmond. We only have three days' supply of food, you know," said Charley.

Ignoring Charley's advice completely, Patrick continued to gnaw on the hard biscuit. "Wonder what the family's name is," he mused to no one in particular.

"Farm is called Garnetts, about five miles east of Richmond," Frank replied. "At least that's what Captain Sweeney and Sergeant O'Toole said."

The boys looked at Frank in amazement and admiration. He always had a way of knowing things.

After a long afternoon of worrisome waiting accompanied by the ongoing noise of battle beyond the river, Jacob Adams tried to reassure the boys of the corps. "I know the waitin' and worryin' is hard, boys. My boy Robby could be over there fightin' the Rebs right now."

"I'd rather be in the thick of it, Jacob," interrupted Frank. "At least then we'd be doin' something instead of sittin' and not knowin'."

"Plenty o' time for that, boy. Plenty o' time," said Jacob.

The sun was a blood red ball dipping low in the sky when suddenly orders flew and men bolted into action.

"Drummers, assemble the regiment!" O'Toole shouted.

Charley left his haversack and all his belongings, except Old Betsy, propped against the wall of the barn. He quickly felt his pocket for Elspeth's forget-me-not pouch and flung the strap of the drum around his neck. His heart pounded, and fresh sweat sprang out across his forehead. He wiped his arm across his eyes and then, along with the rest of the corps, beat out the cadence to call the regiment to battle.

General Winfield Hancock rode tall in his saddle and could be seen above the heads of the soldiers. He spoke encouragements to the men of the regiments and acknowledged their cheers.

Then suddenly an attack was in full swing. Charley, Frank, and Hans stood fast behind the regimental flag, beating their drums while Patrick played his fife. Charley looked at the hardened, set expression on Frank's face and then at Patrick's pale frightened look. He suddenly remembered this was Patrick's first battle! Patrick had sat out the battle of Williamsburg as a prisoner in a Confederate camp! Charley straightened his own shoulders and hardened his face to match Frank's as bullets whizzed by their heads, clipping branches and leaves from the trees.

"Fix bayonets!" The order was shouted as some of the Rebs managed to climb over the stone wall. They were repelled and fell back, only to once more push forward, carried on the wave of a piercing, ear splitting yell like the snarl of a giant beast.

Charley involuntarily took a step back as though to escape the sound of the legendary Rebel yell.

The sky darkened; it was nearly night. The intense fighting quieted as the enemy retreated.

"Drummers, cease!" shouted O'Toole. Charley stopped and slumped to the ground in exhaustion. Echoes of battle hung on the heavy air and rang in Charley's ears. It was soon replaced by the sounds of moaning from the wounded. "Water, water." Cries of "5th Wisconsin", "49th Pennsylvania", "6th Maine", "43rd New York" were heard from men trying to locate their regiments through the smoke and darkness.

Sergeant O'Toole rounded up the drum corps. "Good, lads! No one hurt. Ya did a fine job, all of ya! Now drum out our Pennsylvania 49th call to bring home our brave boys who are lost."

On weary legs the boys of the corps dispersed to obey the command. The somber drum beat, mixed with the moans of the wounded and dying, gave an eerie atmosphere to the field.

*   *   *

Frank watched General Winfield Hancock, astride his horse, gingerly pick his way through the debris of battle. He stopped in the center of the field to survey the scene. Silhouetted in the light of a burning overturned caisson, he dismounted and, placing his arm around the shoulders of a wounded young man, offered him a drink from his own canteen.

Frank stood taller and beat his drum with a stronger rhythm. "There's a real hero. He's not afraid of anything. I sure wish I could be like that. He'd never give up and let go. He'd hang on," Frank mumbled as he fought back tears.

*   *   *

After long hours of carrying wounded and dead from the battlefield, Charley and Frank, too exhausted to pitch a tent, crawled under a caisson and fell asleep on the hard ground. At dawn of June 28, feeling as if they had not rested at all, the boys were immediately dragged into action. A huge, general retreat of the army had begun, and an endless stream of soldiers, wagons, livestock and caissons rumbled past. The soldiers were bewildered and frustrated by the orders to move.

"We held the enemy, didn't we? Why are we retreatin' now? Why not just take Richmond?"

"Little Mac must know what he's doin'," one said. "Maybe we're movin' around the other side of Richmond."

"He sure must know somethin' we don't know because he's got a strange way of doin' things."

The Pennsylvania 49th was part of General Franklin's division. They were among the last to move as part of the rear guard of the Union army, and by evening had marched only a few miles to Golding's farm. Skirmishes throughout the afternoon had forced them to be constantly at ready for battle, never lowering their defenses to rest.

Tediously the men and boys endured. Hancock's brigade reached Savage's Station in mid-afternoon of June 29. By that time the systematic destruction of supplies, which could not be packed and moved quickly enough, was in full swing. Black smoke was sent billowing skyward. Wounded men overflowed from buildings and hospital tents, sprawling on the grass and under trees, to await the surgeons' attention. Wagons, animals, and men moved steadily in the direction of the James River, crowding the narrow roads.

"Look at that!" Patrick said in amazement. "All that food and clothing piled up nearly as high as a building."

"Yeah, just waiting for a match," replied Frank.

"Right, lads," O'Toole shouted above the clatter. "When ya pass the open boxes with blankets, shoes, and trousers, help yourself ta what ya think ya can use. Replenish yer ration of food, but don't overdo it. Remember, what ya take, ya carry."

Fires blazed all around, and the combined aroma of burning coffee, sugar, flour, rice, and pork filled the air.

"Here we are scrambling after a bit of hardtack, and all this good food is burning up for nothing," said Charley.

"Sure ain't fun," said Patrick. "What I wouldn't give to sit down at a proper table full of all that food!"

The magazines of cartridges and kegs of powder and shells were not as easy to dispose of. The boys, chewing on salt pork, watched the last of the excess ammunition loaded into railroad cars with care. Then finally, one by one, the cars were set afire and the long train was put into motion down the track toward the Chickahominy River and the already destroyed bridge. Faster and faster the train sped with the air fanning the flames and spreading the fire to the explosive contents. By the time the train reached the shelter of the forest, huge explosions could be heard with shells shrieking and blazing through the treetops and fragments of the cars tossed high into the sky. And then there was silence after the train had met the river.

The moans of the wounded penetrated the silence. Charley was the first to speak. "We sure aren't leaving anything behind for the Rebs."

"Yeah, nothing but the wounded," replied Frank.

"What? How do you know that?" asked Charley.

"Look, haven't we just been bringing wounded in and leaving them every which way? The surgeons can't begin to take care of this crowd. We sure can't fight and run carrying all of them."

"We wouldn't leave them behind, would we?" asked Patrick, looking at Charley.

No answer came. They simply watched.

Jacob Adams walked among the wounded, peering into faces. To those who were conscious and could answer well enough, he asked the familiar question. Some just turned away. Others looked at him with glazed eyes. One soldier cried, "Mister, don't leave us to the Rebs, I beg of you!"

A figure lay under a blanket, trembling in spite of the heat. All that could be seen above the blanket was a flame of red hair. "Robby, Robby!" Jacob quickened his pace, stepping over bodies strewn in his path. "Robby," he whispered as he knelt on one knee and pulled the blanket from the face of the boy. Blue eyes looked up at him, pleading. In a weak voice through chattering teeth he said, "Sorry, mister, but I'll be Robby if that's what ya want. Just take me with ya. I'll die in a Reb prison camp."

Jacob shook his head, patted the boy's shoulder, and pulled the blanket back up. The boy tried to cling to Jacob's sleeve, but was too weak. In the end, he just turned his head, resigned. Jacob brushed tears from his face and continued his search.

Everywhere officers were paying last visits to their wounded charges. Friends tended friends and made parting promises to write to their families.

"Is this our reward for the battles we have fought and sacrifices we have made?" shouted a soldier to his departing captain.

He struggled to pull himself to his feet. "Sir, sir, do you hear me?"

The captain stopped, visibly struggling, then finally turned and spoke with a trembling voice. "I'm sorry, Daniel. If we take one, we must take you all. And we cannot do that."

By four o'clock in the afternoon, the last of the wagons and troops, except for the rear guard, had departed from Savage's Station with the sun glinting off the guns of the regiments and the banners and music fading from sight and hearing. The Pennsylvania 49th, still as part of the rear defense, was situated on a large plain in front of Savage's Station facing north to stop the advance of the enemy until the Union troops were safely beyond White Oak Swamp.

After an hour of standing in battle formation, they could see a great cloud of dust rising into the air, moving closer and closer. Suddenly the enemy was upon them with that horrifying, piercing yell.

Charley and Frank looked at each other in unspoken communication. Each read the fear and determination on the other's face. They dropped back behind the lines, hardly conscious of the actual orders O'Toole yelled out. They beat a cadence steadily through the heat, the noise, the acrid odor, the smoke, the shells whizzing past. Charley tried to focus on the regimental flag, but his mind wandered. Would it be better to move to dodge the shells or to stand still in hopes the shells would miss him? His heart pounded as hard as his drum, and sweat poured down his face, stinging his eyes. At last, after repeated waves of attack, the enemy retreated, and the fighting ceased as suddenly as it had begun.

The boys automatically began their dismal task of carrying the wounded from the field and deposited them at the soon-to-be abandoned hospital site. Later, exhausted, they sat drinking coffee and awaiting orders.

A messenger approached Captain Sweeney and Sergeant O'Toole who were standing nearby. Captain Sweeney threw his clay pipe to the ground where it shattered against a rock.

Sergeant O'Toole spread his arms palms upward as if seeking an explanation.

"Follow the retreat?" Captain Sweeney exclaimed, "Why don't we just push the enemy right on back into the Chickahominy? It just doesn't make sense. This is a disgrace!" He threw his hat on the ground in disgust and turned his back to the messenger who stood silently with his head down. Sweeney continued to pace, shaking his head.

Sergeant O'Toole finally spoke up. "What are your orders, sir?"

Sweeney, at last resigned, shook his head once more and said evenly, "Continue the retreat, Sergeant. We'll march through the night."

By dawn, the Pennsylvania 49th found themselves at the White Oak Swamp Bridge. The drum corps, having lost touch with all sense of normal existence, dropped their belongings and lay down on the spot to sleep.

After only a few hours of sleep, the regiment was awakened to prepare for still another expected attack from Stonewall Jackson's troops. The White Oak Swamp Bridge, at the narrowest point of the widespread swamp, had been reconstructed only two days earlier by Lieutenant Folwell's 50th New York engineer regiment. Now, after the rear guard passed over the corduroy bridge, it was once again destroyed. Franklin's division was situated along the miserable, marshy edge of the swamp where they clearly watched the enemy set up nearly thirty pieces of artillery on the opposite bank. The Union line of artillery was in turn set in place, and both sides waited tensely and watched.

"Where's their infantry?" Charley asked. "All I can see is their artillery. It doesn't look like they have anyone to back them up."

"Oh, they're there," said Frank knowingly. "Most likely lyin' hidden in all that dense foliage beyond them."

"Yeah," said Patrick. "Who knows how many there are. I'd rather know what we're facin'. I want to see them all spread out on a field."

"And who's going to start this battle?" asked Hans. "Here we are both sittin' and wonderin' who's going to fire the first shot."

On a slight rise between both armies stood a house with an orchard of fruit trees surrounding it. "If we weren't standin' here waitin' for another battle," said Patrick with the ever-present thought of food on his mind, "I'd be up in one of those fruit trees biting into a sweet, juicy peach."

As if the Rebs had heard him speak, a thunderous roar of artillery shook the ground, and the house itself crumbled to its foundation as if sliced by a gigantic cleaver. A moment later, the smoke lifted to reveal only splintered stumps of the orchard.

The cannons thundered at each other across the swamp like giant dragons spitting fire. Finally, after several hours, the firing ceased. The men braced for a Rebel infantry attack which never came. All was quiet except for the rumble of cannon and the sound of shot from a battle engaged further to the west.

The oppressive heat and ever-present mosquitoes forgotten, the boys lay down in any scant shade they could find and soon were lost in exhausted sleep.

"No rest for the weary, lads. On your feet now," O'Toole ordered. The men and boys struggled out of sleep, grumbling and complaining. "Quiet there, quiet. Nothin' between us and the Rebs but that pathetic small bog and burnt-out bridge. So go softly now, or Johnny Reb will be havin' ya for breakfast."

"Frank, are you there?" Charley asked as he stumbled in the darkness following the sound of men in front of him.

"Right here," came the response from just over Charley's right shoulder.

From the other side came Patrick's voice. "I'm here. Hans?"

"Here, too," came the whispered reply.

"All right. Let's stick together and stay awake," Frank said. No further communication was whispered as the company of men and boys plodded through the darkness.

"Horses approaching, horses approaching!" came the alarm from the rear of the column. "Enemy cavalry," someone shouted. "Take cover."

Panic-stricken, the men leapt into the dense, boggy woods on both sides of the narrow road. Charley found himself lying in murky water, barely holding his mouth above the foul-smelling liquid, his heart pounding in anticipation of enemy troops appearing momentarily.

The sound of wheels and hooves grew louder, until coming into view in the barely discernible light of predawn was a single sutler's wagon, rolling along at a trotting pace. A collective sigh arose, along with a few swear words and embarrassed laughter, as the regiment pulled itself from the muddy swamp and poured back onto the narrow road, surrounding the wagon. Losing no time, the startled peddler was dispersing his goods to the highest bidder.

"If he only knew how many rifles were pointed in his direction just now," said Charley.

"Yeah," added Patrick. "He sure wouldn't look so happy."

A piercing yell was suddenly heard above the voices of the men. Then the words, "Snake! Snake!"

Immediately the men moved back in every direction. In the center of the small clearing was Hans jumping around on one foot, holding his other foot in the air and shaking it frantically. A thick snake swung wildly from his boot where its fangs were lodged.

"Get it off! Get it off!" yelled Hans. His face was white in the pale light.

Jacob stepped forward and took Hans firmly by the shoulders. "Hold still, boy. Don't move," he said. Hans still shook his foot uncontrollably.

At the same time, Frank picked up a rifle which had been dropped by the roadside, and holding it by the long barrel, hit at the snake with the butt of the rifle. Finally, its fangs dislodged, the snake fell to the ground, and before it could slither away, another man cut off its head with his bayonet. Then he lifted the body with the sharp tip and flung it back into the dark swamp.

"Are you all right, son? Did it bite you?" asked Jacob.

Before Hans could answer, Sergeant O'Toole was there unlacing and pulling the boot from Hans' foot. "Get some light over here," O'Toole said, "so I can see."

A pine torch was handed over to shine on Hans' bare foot. Though red and blistered from the constant march, no sign of a snake bite could be seen. "Do ya feel pain, lad? Or any numbness or swelling?" O'Toole asked.

Hans, speechless, shook his head.

"Thank God for the thick leather," O'Toole said. Then, "No harm done here. Form up, men, move on, move on!"

Charley took a deep breath as he moved along. "I was in that water with those snakes," he thought. Fearfully, he placed his hand in his pocket and felt for Elspeth's forget-me-not pouch. It was still there, soggy, but with no snake to keep it company.

"I'm getting me a big fat stick," said Hans.

"Yeah, in case we meet that one's big brother!" said Frank.

The others nodded in agreement. They proceeded, carrying drums, haversacks, and big sticks.

The regiments emerged from the smothering humid air of the swamp at sunrise. By full light they had gained higher ground with fields and fields of ripe wheat, rippling golden in the warm breeze from the river. Spirits rose at the sight of the Union gunboats situated on the James River behind them. The bands, after a long imposed silence, struck up "Rally Round the Flag" and "Garry Owen." Carried by the patriotic music, cheers, and flags held high, the Pennsylvania 49th marched through the fields of wheat to Malvern Hill.

The scorching day stretched on. The drum corps' assigned task was to cut and gather wheat into thick sheaves to be used for bedding or food.

"Look at all those fine officers taking their ease in the shade," said Frank, his face beet red from the heat.

"And enjoying glasses of ice water from the old ice house," said Charley.

Hans tasted a handful of wheat grains, but spit out half, unable to swallow the grainy particles. "Hand me my canteen, Patrick," he spoke through a dry mouth.

Patrick didn't answer. He sat with his head slumped forward into his hands.

O'Toole took one look at him and shouted, "Open his shirt. Simpson, you pour that water over him to cool him off. You and you, gather some of those wheat sheaves. Bring them here. Since the officers have left not a whisp of shade for chick nor child, we'll make our own."

Charley and Hans soon gathered enough sheaves of wheat to make a rough shelter which cast a narrow shadow over Patrick. The danger of sunstroke became more of a threat through the long day than the Rebels who were massing in the woods and fields below.

In mid-afternoon the troops were abruptly jolted from their lethargy by the firing of large shells from the Union gunboats in the James River. Soon the heavy Union cannons situated on the summit of Malvern Hill to their rear joined the barrage. The shells whistled low over their heads, barely clearing the Union lines to burst among the trees masking the Confederate troops. Every now and then a volley fell short and exploded in the midst of their own regiments.

"What in blue blazes?" O'Toole shouted as he jumped to his feet. "Isn't it enough the heat and snakes are tryin' to kill us? Now our own boys are havin' a go at it. Move back, lads. Closer to the big guns. Stay low, now. We don't want our nearsighted comrades thinkin' we're the enemy." The corps scrambled quickly to avoid the stray shells.

The booming of the great guns continued, mingled with sharp cracks from Rebel sharpshooters. Then the Confederates opened with their own artillery. At first their balls and shells flew far wide of their target or whizzed so high overhead that they exploded in the air, causing no damage.

Patrick, recovered somewhat from the effects of near sun stroke, said, "Our guns have Johnny Reb so scared, he can't even fire straight."

"Give 'em a few tries and they'll get it right," said Frank. "Those Rebs are plucky fighters."

Frank was right. The grisly guns were soon finding their targets, shells exploding in the midst of the ranks in their deadly mission. Charley watched as a horse and rider were both thrown to the ground. When the smoke and dust cleared, he saw the horse struggle to its feet, the rider gone but his boot and stump of leg still in the stirrup. A month ago the sight would have sickened him, but now in this seventh day of battle after battle, it was just a reality to be endured.

By late afternoon the actual Rebel infantry attack began. The Union troops, entrenched on the hill and surrounding plateau, did not move, but kept up their barrage of fire as wave after wave of Confederates with piercing Rebel yells moved forward in the face of almost certain death. They were ploughed down in rows. No sooner did a gap appear among the ranks of gray and butternut colored uniforms when others emerged from the trees to fill the space.

Cannon, shot, and shell were deafening. Men fell all around. The boys of the corps huddled together, covering their ears with their hands, trying to keep out the pounding of the guns. Charley floated mentally; the shaking of the earth beneath him, the pounding of the guns, the smell of sulphur, the screams of men, all faded as he drifted in his mind. He was walking along the creek with Elspeth, then he was standing in the rain touching her soaked curls, then he was back in West Chester, and it was cool and he could smell the fruit trees in the yard, and . . .

"Charley! . . . Charley . . . " It was Frank, his face right up against him. "Charley!" Frank shouted, shaking him now. "O'Toole says move back. Come on!" Frank grabbed him, pulling him by the arm.

Tripping and reaching for his haversack, Charley ran further to the rear, crouched low. A whistling, earsplitting shell exploded, leaving a deep crater where the boys had been a few moments before. Charley stopped and stared at the spot, mouth open. "Come on!" shouted Frank and tugged once again on Charley's sleeve.

When the full darkness came at last, and both sides could no longer distinguish friend or enemy, the fighting ceased. Triumphant cheers could be heard on the Union side, while the Confederates withdrew, some in groups, some just as lonely stragglers, some trying to help wounded comrades, and others barely managing to get themselves from the field.

Charley stood in the midst of the cheers, but could muster no feeling for it himself. Even in the darkness, lightened only here and there by torches or lanterns like fireflies held aloft by helping hands, he could feel more than see the incredible number of bodies. The pocked field literally moved and wept as if human itself. The cries and moans of the wounded were so many that the sounds were almost as deafening as the guns had been earlier.

Frank stood by his side and seemed to share what Charley was feeling. "In all the battles we've seen this past week, this has been the worst," he said in a low voice.

Charley nodded. "More like murder than war," he said.

Already thousands of troops were moving out. "Where to now?" Patrick asked incredulously. "Haven't we just won this battle? Aren't we going to stand fast or take Richmond?"

An older soldier passing by overheard and said, "It's a disgrace, son, a disgrace. Seeing as how you're not an officer I'll go so far as to call Little Mac a coward. Running scared and expecting the whole army to follow like yellow dogs with their tails between their legs!" He shook his head in disgust and passed on.

Frank raised a lantern high and the light fell upon a wounded man, and the boys went to work. Placing the soldier on top of a blanket, Charley took one end and Frank the other. They carried their moaning cargo back to the waiting wagons for transport overland to the hospital ships on the James River. They repeated this routine for the next hour. Exhausted, they no longer knew if their heavily laden blanket-stretchers carried dead or wounded, and they cared very little either way.

The smells and the sounds of pain were almost overwhelming, but somehow, above it all, or perhaps separate from it all, Charley's ear caught a refrain sung by a familiar voice. "Over here, Frank," he said and pulled him by the sleeve to follow the sound.

"We'd call to the stars to keep out of our way; Lest we should rock over their toes. And there we would stay till the end of the day and on the next rainbow come home."

Jacob Adams sat, cradling a still form in his arms. He rocked back and forward singing softly as if lulling a baby to sleep. The glow of lantern light shone upon the red hair of the boy held in Jacob's embrace. "And on the next rainbow come home," the baritone voice repeated lowly.

"Jacob, Jacob," Charley spoke. "Let us take him for help. He's bleeding."

"Come home," Jacob sang again, his eyes, filled with tears, stared straight ahead.

"I'm binding up his leg. Stop him from rockin' so much," Frank said.

"Jacob," Charley spoke again. "Let us help him."

"He's gone. My Robby's gone." Jacob spoke so softly that they could scarcely hear him. "I found him too late."

"No, Jacob. He'll be all right if you'd just let us get him some help. Look, he's trying to open his eyes," Frank said.

Jacob bent his head over Robby's face. Then he stared up at Frank in disbelief. "He said 'Pa.' I heard him!"

Robby was placed upon the stretcher blanket. Jacob held the lantern aloft and led the way to the wagons. Seeing Sergeant O'Toole, Jacob fairly shouted, "I found him, Michael. And he's alive! Robby's alive!"

"Aye, I see ya have, Jacob."

"I need to go along in the wagon, Michael, or he'll never survive." Then, lowering his voice, he said, "He's all that I have left."

"Well, I'll not say ya can go, Jacob, and I'll not say ya musn't. If I was ta be occupied with other endeavors at the time, sure I'd not notice all comin's and goin's." Then, turning his back to the wagon and walking away, Sergeant O'Toole said, "Come on, lads. Form up to move out."

As the wagon, filled with wounded men, pulled away, no one questioned the gray-bearded man sitting with a pale, red haired boy cradled in his arms.

Chapter Thirteen

Harrison's Landing, Virginia ——— July and August, 1862

They were back on the road again, plodding along through the dark as they had done all week—marching by night, resting but a few hours in the morning, fighting all afternoon and evening, no food rations left. Only this time it was worse. Sometime in the early dark hours of the morning of July 2 a steady rain had started, and before long the dusty road had churned to a sea of mud. All sense of order seemed lost. Men from countless different regiments streamed silently side by side along the road and through the woods and fields. When their arms grew too tired to carry their burdens, they simply dropped their rifles, haversacks, and anything else to the ground as they unheedingly passed the mud-bogged wagons and herds of cattle. Their destination was Harrison's Landing on the James River—a mere eight miles from Malvern Hill, but a seemingly endless journey to the battle-weary and footsore soldiers.

Somehow Sergeant O'Toole kept the boys of the drum corps together, but they lost the rest of the Pennsylvania 49th. Charley kept hold of Old Betsy under his makeshift oilcloth cover, but didn't remember when or where he had dropped his haversack.

The overanxious men of the engineer corps ahead of them had already cut and leveled trees haphazardly across the single River Road, supposedly to halt the progress of the enemy. The only progress they were halting was of their own troops. Thousands of candles, lanterns, and bonfires burned fitfully along the road in the steady rain, providing an eerie false daylight effect. Here and there an abandoned wagon was set afire, sparks hissing.

The dismal light of day did nothing to cheer the mob of men. It served only to reveal the bedraggled and confused state of the entire Union Army of the Potomac in the now torrential rain. The combined smell of unwashed lice-infested bodies, wet filthy wool uniforms, blood and festering wounds, mud, and thousands of animals and their excrement was all encompassing.

Late in the morning they emerged from woods to the vast, muddy plain bordering the river.

"Look at the ships!" Patrick exclaimed. The other boys followed his direction. Sure enough, masts and smokestacks of a flotilla of at least a hundred ships could be clearly seen.

"Here at last," Hans muttered.

"Yeah, but where are we to go?" said Charley. He looked around at the even greater chaos of the hopelessly mingled regiments.

"Follow me," O'Toole ordered. The bedraggled group slumped along behind him as he made his way to an officer. O'Toole saluted and then spoke to the major, who stood disgruntled in the downpour with an oilskin wrapped about him, a large hat with water dripping from the brim, and yellow hair plastered against wet forehead and face.

"Why, it's old golden curls," Frank said. "He sure don't look too pretty today."

"This way for the sixth corps, Hancock's division." The major pointed to his left.

O'Toole nodded. "Come along, lads. And cut ya'selves any vestige of wheat ya can find to put between ya'selves and the mud. It's a bed ya'll be wantin'."

They followed him across the trampled and foraged wheat field. Finally they stopped at a designated area and, placing in the mud what few stalks of wheat they had gleaned, they literally fell on top of them. Ignoring the rain which trickled into their ears and down their necks, they curled into some semblance of comfort, wrapped in oilcloth.

Just before sleep came, Frank said almost to himself, "Naw, he sure don't look too pretty today."

Both he and Charley smiled. Before he closed his eyes, Charley thought, "We haven't smiled in a long time."

The boys slept soundly for a full twenty-four hours. Charley finally awoke to sun and warmth and the tantalizing aroma of pork roasting, coffee brewing, and bread baking. The mass chaos of the day before had changed to an actual camp setting. A mess tent was up and the cooks were busy with the new supplies brought in on the flotilla.

"Well, well, lads." O'Toole grinned when one by one the boys crawled from their makeshift beds. "So ya see fit to join the world again. Come on now, get some food in ya."

They were ravenous. Patrick tore into his bread and bit a hunk of pork, hardly taking time to chew before he swallowed and bit into more. "Best bacon I ever tasted," he said through a mouth filled with food.

Charley, on the other hand, savored each bite. He resisted the initial greedy impulse and tasted the juicy morsels of salty pork, the dry, crusty bread, the warm tender beans, and even enjoyed the steaming, unsweetened coffee to wash it all down. But more than anything, he could not get enough of the cool, clear spring water. He gulped down cup after cup as if it cleansed his whole system of the endless smoke and dust of battle.

"Hey, leave some for us whales," laughed Frank.

Finally, thirst quenched and stomachs full, Sergeant O'Toole tossed them each a rough bar of soap. "Head for the river, lads, and give ya'selves a good scrub. Toss those rags o' uniforms in the fire. Here's some new finery, compliments of the United States government. It's fresh and clean from the skin out ya'll be." Open crates containing new uniforms lay at O'Toole's feet.

They stripped down to their drawers. Charley felt in all his pockets, retrieving Grandpa Eb's knife, his precious forget-me-not pouch from Elspeth, and his last letter from home, damp and crumpled. "Sergeant O'Toole, will you hold these for me?" he asked.

"Sure, lad, sure," he said resignedly and held out his hand. "Any other treasures ta be put in safe keepin'?" he asked the others.

Charley tossed his uniform onto the fire as the others had done. "I hope all the lice bake to a crisp," he said laughing.

The boys pushed and shoved each other as they ran free of the hot, heavy uniforms. They dove ecstatically into the wide creek that emptied into the river. Much of the regiment was there before them, and men of all ages were laughing, splashing, lathering and scrubbing, throwing water, and dunking their fellow soldiers. The water foamed from the soap and swept away the grime and filth of the past weeks.

Sitting on the grassy bank in the warm sun, the boys relaxed. "Who's for another swim?" Patrick asked as he headed back to the water.

"Me," said Hans. "Can't get cool enough after that smothering swamp."

"Watch out for snakes," Frank called after him. Then he said to Charley, "We need to pitch our tent in case it rains again to-night."

"Yeah, and collect some writing supplies so we can write home," replied Charley. As soon as he spoke, he was sorry.

"Ain't got anybody to write home to, . . . or even a home."

"I m sorry, Frank. I forgot."

"Well, it's no matter," Frank said with a shrug.

"How'd you join up with no address?" Charley asked.

"All right, I'll tell you," Frank said. "Remember when I was on the train?"

"When you lost your sister, Meg?"

"After that. It was a long ride on the train, and when it slowed to pull into Philadelphia, I jumped off. Thought I'd get me a job. I was walkin' down a street when I saw a policeman on the other side. I pulled my cap down low over my face, but he stopped, put his hands behind his back, and rocked back and forth from toe to heel, all the while starin' at me. I knew the people from the orphan asylum would be searchin' for me, so I looked around and ducked into a store front. It was a recruitin' station. When they asked me if I wanted to be a drummer, I said, 'sure,' and here I am. But when I get out next year, I'm goin' back to find Meg, and we will be a family!"

"I'll help you find her, Frank."

By the fourth of July a huge, orderly encampment had developed at Harrison's Landing. Tent cities had sprung up with wide "streets" running from the river across the plain. Hospital ships carried wounded to safety in the North, and supply ships provided fresh food and supplies for the thousands of men. General McClellan went all out to lift the morale of his army. He rode through all the camps amidst loud cheers, and he issued a stirring message which was read aloud to each regiment. It ended:

> On this our nation's birthday we declare to our foes . . . that the Union, which can alone insure internal peace and external security to each state, must and shall be preserved, cost what it may in time, treasure, and blood.

Charley, having found paper, pen, and ink, wrote to his family.

> I had fresh fruit today. Never has an apple tasted sweeter. Since today is our nation's birthday, we took our ease. After a swim in the river, we had a parade, and the

guns fired a salute at high noon. General McClellan rode up and down our ranks, and we all cheered heartily.

What I have seen over these past days since I last wrote, I cannot explain. I don't know when it happened, but to see a dead man now is no different to me than seeing a dead chicken or slaughtered hog. I was very nearly a slaughtered hog myself. But for my friend, Frank Simpson, I would not be here. He pulled me from danger to safety with very little time to spare. Mama and Papa, he has no family of his own. Only a sister he has lost. After this war is over he will try to find her. Perhaps, Papa, you could find work for him in your shop, and together we can help him search for his sister.

We have received new uniforms since we arrived here, though not so fine as yours, Papa, and the fit is loose. Sergeant O'Toole says we will be here for a time, so if you wish to send me mail, I am sure it will reach me.

Hello to all my brothers and sisters. Write soon.

Your loving son,
Charles

When darkness fell on the evening of the fourth, the lights from countless glimmering campfires lit up the surrounding plain. That, along with the lights of the flotilla bobbing at anchor in the river and along the quickly constructed wharves gave Harrison's Landing the look of a long established seaport.

Invigorated by fresh food, the men of the company contentedly sat around the campfire smoking and singing, "Hurrah for the wagon! The old Union wagon! We'll stick to our wagon, And we'll all take a ride." From out of the darkness beyond the light of the fire a strong baritone voice joined in "For the good old Union wagon was the glory of the world."

O'Toole smiled and without turning around, shifted his position, leaving a space next to him. Still singing, Jacob Adams entered the circle of light and seated himself. Charley stopped singing and leaned forward. He opened his mouth as if to speak to Jacob, but a warning glance from O'Toole prevented him. The group continued the song, and Jacob Adams was once again part of the regiment, his absence unnoticed or unmentioned.

After the others had gone and the campfire was burning low, Charley and Frank remained with Sergeant O'Toole and Jacob Adams. Jacob looked different somehow, his gray beard was trimmed neatly to just below his chin, his uniform new and clean, but it was more than that, Charley thought. Jacob smiled and laughed with Sergeant O'Toole as he had not done in a long while.

Frank asked, "How is your son, Jacob?"

"He's doing well, Frank, thanks to your quick action in binding up that wound, and thanks to the kind women of the sanitary commission who doctored him. Those angels of mercy say he'll have a limp, maybe, but not lose his leg. If you boys had not helped him . . . I hate to think. . . . I am in your debt."

Frank and Charley looked at each other, not knowing what to say.

"Robby has seen the elephant, that's for sure," Jacob added, shaking his head slowly.

"What do you mean, Jacob?" Charley asked. "I've wondered about that since you first said it back in Lewinsville."

"Well, boys, it's like this. When the circus comes to town with all the animals and the acrobats and calliope music, the excitement fills the air, and every boy wants to be part of it. Why, he'd do just about anything for the price of a ticket. Many a farm boy has been shocked when he got his wish to work his way into a circus tent. A bucket and shovel sure isn't much help once he's seen the elephant's size. It's bigger and much more dangerous than he ever imagined. Well, now you've all seen the elephant. Things are not always as glorious as they seem at first."

"Right, lads," O'Toole spoke in a firm voice which by its tone dismissed them. They stood, said good night, and left the older men to their pipes.

The following week Charley, Frank, Hans, and Patrick, carrying bundles of laundry, approached the small community of tents near the river's edge where abandoned or escaped slaves had taken refuge. Pots of boiling water hung on makeshift tripods over fires, as women pushed the contents deeper into the simmering water with long poles. Clothes hung on tree limbs and bushes, bleaching and drying in the hot July sun. Barefoot children ran among the boiling kettles, heedless of the heat and the danger. Women laughed and gossiped among themselves. Somewhere a harmonica played.

Charley handed his bundle of clothes to a woman. "Yes, mister. You come back this time tomorrow. It'll be all cleaned for you."

When Charley turned to leave, he heard a tin-sounding drum beat coming from the direction of the nearby tents. "Listen," he said to Patrick. "What's that?"

Patrick cocked his head to one side and listened, then laughed. "It's blasted bangin', that's what."

As Frank and Hans joined them, Patrick motioned toward the sound. "Well, it sure isn't any drum major, but it's got a beat," said Frank.

While they stood there, the banging grew louder. "Awwww," Patrick covered his ears. Just then from behind one of the tents a small boy marched. His bare feet kicked up dust as he raised his knees high. An upside-down bucket hung from a rope around his neck. He held two stout sticks and beat a marching cadence on the old tin bucket. Bang, bang, bang! He came closer, an old hat pushed back on his head, smiling, eyes sparkling.

"Joseph!" Charley shouted. "Look, it's Joseph!"

The boys surrounded the little drummer, laughing and talking all at once.

"I been practicin', mister. Hear that tune? I been practicin'."

By the time they returned to their posts, it had been decided that Joseph would help the corps with delivering the company's laundry in return for daily drumming lessons, as time would permit, of course.

President Lincoln himself had come to review the troops on July 8! The news travelled faster than a telegraph wire throughout the regiments. Orders were to spruce up the camps and dress in full uniform. For nearly two hours, the drum corps stood in position with drums at hand, waiting. They could hear the drum rolls, the regimental bands, the cheers come progressively closer as Lincoln paid his respects to each individual regiment in turn.

"Do you think your grand friend will remember you?" Frank asked. It was the nearest tone to sarcasm that he had used in a long time.

Charley shrugged his shoulders. He thought back to early March, a mere four months, but it seemed years ago. Charley felt much older now. "I know one thing, I won't be tossing any batons in the air this time."

Frank grinned.

When the president and his entourage finally approached the Pennsylvania 49th, Charley stood as tall as he could and proudly beat Old Betsy. Little Mac was straight and at ease in the saddle on his dark bay horse. The president looked too large for his mount, his long bony knees thrust forward from the stirrups and his elbow bent back like stiff grasshopper legs. Charley felt a lump rise in his throat. He remembered this kind, tall man bending to him and whispering, "Your baton tossing requires a bit more practice." Now Charley beat his drum even harder, straightened his back even more, and looked directly ahead. The president took off his hat and waved it just as he came in front of the corps. Charley thought he saw a glimmer of recognition in Mr. Lincoln's eyes as his glance swept over the men of the Pennsylvania 49th.

Late in the evening Charley, Frank, and Patrick managed to make their way down to the wharf to watch the president board his steamer *Ariel*. A group of former slaves stood silently along the river edge. Bareheaded, President Lincoln nodded to them just as he had saluted all the regiments earlier.

The days fell into a routine, and what had seemed luxury to the boys during the first week—sleeping, eating, bathing in the rivers—quickly changed to monotony. Daily drills in 100 degree heat in their hot wool uniforms for the benefit of a few disinterested officers seemed far different from the grand spectacles they had put on for families, sweethearts, and politicians back during the defense of Washington. And even worse were the flies. Hordes of black, stinging flies had swarmed into camp, perhaps drawn by the open latrines and the discarded remains of the animals which the butchers neglected to bury. But they were not limited to these odorous areas. They were everywhere—blackening the tents, ready to drop into a cup of coffee or light on every spoonful of food, buzzing in their ears at night or biting the backs of their necks when they tried to sleep.

Charley spent most of his free time writing letters home and to Elspeth. And each day the busy mail boats, which arrived heavily laden at the wharf, brought quick replies and parcels. Mama and Papa wrote by return mail.

My Dear Charles,

> We are thankful that God has seen fit to spare you. We pray for you daily. Of course your kind friend, Frank Simpson, will always have a place in our grateful hearts and be welcome in our home. We thank the Lord that he was nearby and had the presence of mind to help you! But, Charles, Captain Sweeney promised us you would not be in danger. The newspaper accounts of the Seven Days Battle were horrifying, and our only peace of mind was in knowing you would not be in line of fire. We pray that you will keep close to Captain Sweeney's protection. . . ."

Captain Sweeney's protection! Charley almost laughed. He hardly had any contact with Captain Sweeney!

Mama had packed a parcel of two shirts, new underdrawers, and raisin cakes wrapped in brown paper. Also tucked into the top was a second letter, addressed to Master Frank Simpson from Adeline and Pennell King.

"Here's a letter for you," Charley said.

Frank looked up from his boot-polishing. "Me?" His eyes were bright, then suspicious. "Who would write to me?"

"My folks would," Charley replied.

Frank took the letter, his hands shaking. He stuffed it into his pocket. "I'll read it later," he said, trying to appear indifferent. "Goin' down to the supply tent. I need more polish," Frank said as he placed a half full tin of boot black on the ground and hurried from the tent.

"I do believe it's the first letter he ever got," said Patrick.

*   *   *

Frank was so moved, so proud to receive a letter! But now, what was he to do with it? How could he admit he couldn't even read it? He knew he could ask Charley to read it aloud to him, and Charley would do it willingly. But all the boys were beginning to look up to him now, including Charley, and he did not want to lower himself in their estimation. Charley could read and write so well, and even Patrick in his less learned ways. No, he couldn't ask them, but he could ask Jacob. Jacob would not think any less of him for his lack of learning.

Frank made his way in the opposite direction of the supply tent to where Jacob Adams leaned against a tree. . . .

They wanted him to come and live with them when enlistment was up! A real home and a real job and a real family! Frank could not believe his ears.

Jacob read on in a steady voice, ". . . most welcome here. My husband and Charles will do all in their power to help you locate your lost sister."

The words washed over Frank like a welcoming, cooling shower. Oh, he'd work hard. He'd be the best worker Mr. King ever had. But first he'd find Meg. "We" will find Meg. It sounded good to say "we," to have help, someone else who cared! He turned the phrase over in his mind, testing it. "We will find her." Good, good.

"Frank." It was Jacob's voice. "Here's your letter. Good luck to you! It sounds like you have a bright future!"

"Yeah, thanks, Jacob." Frank rose, folded the letter and placed it in his pocket. He slowly walked back to the tent and his friend.

"Have some raisin cake," Charley offered when Frank returned. "My mama's a good cook, but you'll find that out when we go home."

Frank held his hand out to receive his cake. Tears brimmed in his eyes as he said, "Yeah, when we go home."

*   *   *

Charley spent hours writing to Elspeth. Somehow when he was writing to her or reading her weekly replies, he felt as if they were actually speaking.

. . . Our VI Corps has been relocated to Evelynton Heights. It's on higher ground and we have a view of the whole camp all the way down to the James River with all the gunboats and supply ships. I am working on a map so that when we meet again, I can show you all the places I've been. The big Berkeley House was once a grand mansion, but now all the fine trees surrounding it have been felled and signal towers built on the roof. The inside is a hospital, and General McClellan has set up his headquarters on the lawn. Each morning at dawn or in the evening, depending on the wind, Professor Lowe launches his balloon.

The flies are a terrible nuisance. As I write, I have been eating a raisin cake which Mama sent me. But now I see the "raisins" have multiplied a thousand times. It is covered with so many black flies, big flies, little flies, and in between flies that I think it will soon take wing and fly out of the tent. . . .

The boys had built a shelter of tree limbs over the tent in an effort to keep out the heat of the day, but it did very little to cool the tent by nightfall. They lay in the uncomfortable heat, trying to sleep. From down below, the regimental bugler started to play. It was not the familiar "Extinguish Lights." Each note, crystal clear and haunting, hung on the night air. Movement slowed and even the card games were interrupted as men turned toward the sound. Other company buglers in turn repeated the melody. Lanterns all over the camp were extinguished as the final notes drifted away to leave only the night sounds of insects and frogs.

"What was that bugle call?" Charley asked in a low voice.

"It's called 'Taps,'" Hans answered. "I heard General But- terfield's bugler play it the other day."

"It sure is pretty," Patrick added.

"Sounds lonesome," said Frank.

Just after midnight on August 1, the sound of cannon fire roared through the sultry night air. The Union troops rolled out of their tents to see shells exploding high overhead.

Charley stood rubbing sleep from his eyes. "Looks like the Rebs are trying to sink our supply ships," he said.

"But they are nowhere near. Those little guns can't shoot all across this river," said Patrick.

"It sure does look pretty from up here, though," Charley replied as they watched the fireworks display from the vantage point of Evelynton Heights. It was soon over and without much damage.

As they rolled back into their tents, swatting at the ever-pres- ent flies, Frank grumbled, "It would be worth it if the cannon killed some of these flyin' vermin."

Instead of providing a chance for the Union army to grow healthier, the long encampment at Harrison's Landing caused hundreds more men to become sick. The supply of pure water was short-lived, and more and more men drank contaminated water from the river and streams. The sanitary conditions of so many people living in such a small area with open latrines were terrible. Each day more of the sick were evacuated on hospital ships. That, and the systematic removal of supplies started rumors among the frustrated troops. Did this signal the beginning of a new attack on Richmond or the retreat back down the peninsula to Fort Monroe? During the week between August 8 and August 15, they were left in a sort of limbo. At one point they were told to pack their tents and prepare three days' food rations, only to be left exposed to the hot sun all day and then to sleep under the open sky at night. Finally on August 16 the general retreat began.

"I guess this is better than just being left here in Virginia to burn to a crisp," said Hans.

"Well, at least here we got enough to eat," said Patrick. "I sure don't want to go back to an empty stomach and tired feet."

They began the slow march, this time on dry roads choked with dust.

"Look at those," Charley pointed to some infantry men who were propping logs between wheels to look like cannons and then wrapping them in rubber blankets. Some other men were stuffing straw into blue uniforms to make scare crow sentries. "Quaker guns. Isn't that what Jacob called them?"

"Yeah," Frank nodded. "But somehow, I don't think they'll fool the Rebs."

Along the side of the road Joseph stood, watching the departure of the troops. Gone was the makeshift bucket, and hanging in its place in front of Joseph was a standard issue drum, which Jacob Adams had appropriated for him. As Charley came into his view, Joseph reached up and pulled off his tattered hat, holding it in front of his chest. Charley smiled and lifted his drum sticks high in salute.

Chapter Fourteen

The Maryland Campaign —— September, 1862

Just under two weeks later the Pennsylvania 49th found itself back in Centreville, Virginia. The days had been a systematic retracing of their steps back over the Chickahominy River, this time at a wide point on a bobbing, hastily-constructed pontoon bridge which was disassembled quickly after the Union troops crossed over. Then on through Williamsburg, past Yorktown, and back to Fort Monroe where they reboarded an assortment of ships to steam back up the Chesapeake Bay and Potomac River. The return trip lacked the excitement and anticipation of victory which had carried them down. But for Charley it held the hope of going home, at least closer to home, to a more familiar lay of land, and nearer to Elspeth.

The sturdy log huts of Centreville provided shelter and shade from the hot northern Virginia summer. Supplies and mail caught up with the men. The persistent sutlers rolled into the encampment, peddling their wares to the men at exorbitant prices.

"Every time I hear a peddler wagon clank and bang its pots and pans, I hope it will be Mr. Sinclair with El sitting up there beside him," said Charley to Frank.

"I don't think that poor old mule Nelson could pull the wagon this far," laughed Frank.

"I wrote to El and told her we were headed up her way, so maybe . . ." He did not finish the sentence.

"Charley," Frank spoke. They were sitting in the shade on a bench up against the log hut. "When we get home to Pennsylvania, are you really going to help me find Meg?"

"Sure I am, and Papa, too. He knows lots of people, being that he's in business and all. Mama and Papa are looking forward to meeting you. Don't be nervous about it, you'll see."

A second Battle of Bull Run raged near Manassas, not far from Centreville, and the boys could hear the booming guns and see the clouds of smoke rising. The Pennsylvania 49th was held at ready, but were not engaged in battle. Finally after the disheartening sight of defeated columns of retreating Union troops, they were called in to cover the withdrawal to Fairfax Court House in case the Confederates pursued.

Remembering the rioting, destructive troops of last March, the townspeople of Fairfax Court House closed and barred their homes and farms. Charley and Frank made their way to the house of Horace and his grandmother where they had been welcomed before.

The house looked deserted. All the windows were shuttered, and nothing stirred. A board squeaked as the boys crossed the front porch. It was the only sound. Charley knocked on the door. No response, so he knocked again. They heard the sound of a door close softly inside the house.

"It's Charley and Frank. Remember us?" they called.

No response came. "Come on. We're not welcome here," said Frank.

"But we helped Horace and his grandma," Charley said.

"Yeah, we helped them with their calf. Then the army helped themselves to calf and cow. To them, we're all the enemy."

"I suppose that's true," Charley agreed.

Within days they had pulled closer into Washington almost to the site of their original Lewinsville encampment. Charley hastily wrote to Elspeth and put the letter in the mail. If only he could get away to find her house, he was sure he could get to her faster than the mail wagon would. Elspeth was constantly on his mind, and whatever he was doing, he was always alert to the comings and goings of wagons and townspeople.

On September 5 rumors flew that General Lee's troops had crossed into Maryland, and a flurry of preparations began. This time the Union troops would be in pursuit again rather than humiliating retreat, and the general morale rose immediately.

Early the morning of September 6, Charley drummed the regiment into formation to begin their march into Maryland. Almost frantic now that they were leaving and he had not seen Elspeth, Charley's eyes kept scanning the crowd instead of watching where his feet led. He stumbled over a cobbled street.

"King! Eyes ahead!" bellowed Sergeant O'Toole.

Charley obeyed reluctantly, but as he turned his head he thought he glimpsed a small figure above the crowd, standing on the seat of a wagon, golden hair gleaming in the sun. When they turned the corner, he shot a quick glance back to his left. He saw the figure again, this time with hand raised. He raised his own drumstick high in the air for a fleeting second. "It was Elspeth," he told himself. "It had to be."

The advance into Maryland was invigorating. The weather had cooled some, and the countryside was very much like Pennsylvania with its rolling hills, mountains in the distance, and well-kept farms lined with dry stonewalls and with handsome stone or brick houses. Best of all, they were no longer considered the enemy by the local people. True, Maryland was a border state and had its share of Southern sympathizers, but it seemed to Charley that most of the people in the small towns they passed through or bivouacked near were friendly. They freely offered fresh water from their wells and sold them produce at a fair price.

"Sure didn't join this man's army to be a mountain climber," Patrick complained as the Pennsylvania 49th climbed the steep winding road up the side of Sugarloaf Mountain on September 10.

"Well, it's better than the swamp and the snakes," said Hans.

"And the flies," Frank chimed in.

Charley said nothing as he trudged through the misty drizzle.

The men made camp high above the surrounding countryside. The rain stopped, and the sky cleared. A slash of red sunset lit the western sky.

"It's pretty here, once it clears up," said Hans.

"Yes, it makes me think of the Pennsylvania mountains," replied Charley. "I'll wager I could see clear to Pennsylvania from the signal tower over there. What's that town down below? See the spires of the churches? It looks like West Chester."

"That's Frederick," replied Jacob Adams. "Maybe we'll be down there ourselves in a day or so."

"Yeah, since we're chasin' the Rebs at last," agreed Patrick.

That night campfires burned on the mountain top as the soldiers sang songs of love and home and watched the lights of Frederick glitter in the distance below. "Aura Lee, Aura Lee, all my dreams fulfill . . ." Charley lay in his tent and listened to the voices of the men singing. The music drifted on the clear mountain air. "Sunlight gleams on Aura Lee . . ." He fell asleep thinking of sunlight gleaming on golden hair.

"We sure do fill up a town in a hurry," Frank said as the Union troops proceeded through the narrow street of Burkittsville on September 14. "All I can see ahead of us are soldiers and all I can see behind us are more soldiers."

"I hope these farmers have some good food to sell," said Patrick.

"Don't you ever think of anything but food? Can't you hear the church bells yonder? It's the Sabbath," said Hans. "No buying or selling on a Sunday."

"Huh," mumbled Patrick. "Have to tell my stomach it's a Sunday."

The mention of the Sabbath reminded Charley of a more placid life of habits and traditions. Mama and Papa would be listening to bells as they walked arm in arm to church with his brothers and sisters following behind. "A parade of Kings," Grandpa Eb had called the Sunday ritual. Charley smiled at the memory.

"What are you grinnin' about, King?" Frank's question was abruptly cut short by the whiz overhead of shot, slicing limbs of trees and showering the men with leaf and branch.

"Drummers to the rear, thirty paces!" O'Toole shouted. The boys were already running, heads down, toward the rear of the column.

"Stay to the left of the road!" Captain Sweeney shouted. "Our division is in the lead, men. It's up to you!"

Charley and Frank and Hans maintained an uphill doubletime march, beating the cadence for advance. Suddenly it seemed much hotter to Charley, and his breath came in short spurts, tugging at his lungs. His mouth was as dry as cotton and his heart pounded, but strangely he wasn't scared. All he could think of was the steep, wooded climb and keeping up the pace. This was so different from the flat lands of the peninsula battles. Shots flew through the woods, striking trees and men, but still the pace continued.

Now a stone wall hindered the progress. A wave of blue coated men swept over, then another and another until it was Charley's and Frank's and Hans' and Patrick's turn. Charley looked to the right and saw Frank throw his drum over the wall and then fling himself quickly after it. Patrick, the fifer, followed easily without the hindrance of a drum. On his left, Hans was struggling over while holding on to his drum. He'll be up on the wall too long that way, Charley thought. A good target for a Reb sharpshooter.

"Throw the drum over first!" he shouted to Hans, but his voice could not carry through the din of battle.

Charley flung "Old Betsy" ahead of him and scrambled as quickly as he could to the other side. He could not see Frank through the smoke, but saw the company flag. He took up his position and began again to beat out a steady cadence. Soon through the gunfire and shouting, he heard Frank's steady drumbeat to his right. Then the rhythm was joined from the left.

"Hans made it!" Charley shouted in Frank's direction. He knew Frank could not hear him, but it made him feel better, somehow, to shout it out loud.

Finally they reached the crest. Large groups of Rebel prisoners stood clustered together. They looked haunted, Charley thought, and lost and hungry. There was a piece of captured artillery and stands of captured arms to the other side of the sign lettered "Crampton's Gap, South Mountain."

Still there was no chance to rest. The Pennsylvania 49th kept moving, down this time, and on toward the valley in pursuit of the retreating enemy. By nightfall the fighting ceased.

"'Tis the natural end of battle when a man can no longer see his enemy," Sergeant O'Toole commented to the drummers. "A man starts to long for darkness and despise the light of day in war."

The Pennsylvania 49th hastily made camp in the pleasant valley outside the town of Rohrersville. For once, the drummer boys were not called upon to remove the dead and wounded from the battlefield. "Must be other drummers from the division doin' the job tonight," Charley commented to Frank.

"We surely did show the Rebs a thing or two today," Jacob Adams spoke softly to no one in particular as the men sat by the campfire that night.

Charley nodded his head. "Yes, I never saw so many prisoners or captured guns," he said.

Patrick lay sprawled on the ground, sleeping by the fire. Frank had gone to sleep hours ago, but Charley could not.

"You lot did a yeoman's job out there today, King. Ya must be expirin' with the lack o' rest. Wrap up now, and sleep while ya can."

Obeying Sergeant O'Toole, Charley rolled up in his blanket. He thought he would not sleep. However, he remembered nothing until O'Toole nudged him with the toe of his boot the next morning. "Up, lads, up. Time ta beat out reveille."

At first light on September 17 Charley and Frank huddled around the campfire and sipped their coffee. They watched the trees emerge from indistinct blackness to become dark silhouettes against the gray sky. Patrick appeared, grinning from ear to ear and carefully carrying his tin cup which brimmed with a thick amber substance.

"Got a real treat for us today!" he shouted. "Look! It's honey! A friend of mine from the 6th Maine paid a visit to a farmer's beehive last night. Sweetest thing I've had since Ma's apple pie."

Charley scooped the honey out on a piece of hardtack and ate it slowly, savoring the sweetness and licking his lips and fingertips afterwards. "These old hard biscuits never have tasted so good!"

"Yeah, Patrick, for once I'm glad you have such a good appetite. You're a great one for sniffin' out the food," said Frank. He took a spoonful and stirred it into his coffee. "Always did prefer my rye sweetened," he added.

As the gray misty dawn filled the sky, a single cannon fire rumbled to the west and north of them, and others quickly answered.

"It's comin' from Hagerstown way from the sound of it," said Jacob who had joined the boys for a taste of honey.

"That's right next door to Pennsylvania!" said Patrick. "Our boys'll have to stop the Rebs soon before they get clear up to Maine."

"Yeah, 'Our boys' means us, too," said Charley.

"Drummers, sound assembly!" came the order.

"And here we go," muttered Frank as he rushed with the others to play the long roll.

By six a.m. the Pennsylvania 49th had passed through the small village of Rohrersville. Charley looked back toward the long ridge of South Mountain, but it was lost in a fog of low-lying clouds. The air was close and humid.

At mid-morning the men rested on a hilltop outside of Keedysville. The sun had burned away the low-lying clouds, and now from their vantage they had a clear view of the battle raging in the fields beyond the creek below them. No one spoke much. In silent accord the soldiers began to throw their playing cards to the ground. Only four months ago the scattered cards had puzzled Charley, but now it was just another familiar sign of battle. After all, if it were a man's time to die, he did not want a deck of cards sent home to his sweetheart or mother along with his other belongings. No need to have them remember him as a gambler.

General Hancock rode along the line of men and stopped to speak. "Boys, do as you have before. Be brave and true, and I think this will be your last battle."

The regiment burst into cheers, but Frank said with a nudge to Charley, "Does he mean our last battle or the last battle of the war?"

Charley didn't answer.

Now ordered forward again, the regiment splashed through the creek. In the middle it was thigh-deep, and Charley hoisted "Old Betsy" to his chest, his arms clasped around the drum. Something, not solid like a rock or branch, bumped his leg and hindered his movement. Charley pushed away with his knee, but the thing seemed to wrap around him in response. He looked down to his side and, in instant revulsion, he saw that the hindrance was a body lying face down, its hair floating around its head in a bloody red halo. An arm had wrapped around Charley's leg. Involuntarily, Charley kicked out again to free himself, and with that movement a fresh flow of blood seeped crimson from the dead man's wound.

"Keep movin'! Keep movin'!" the soldiers behind Charley growled as they stumbled forward across Antietam Creek.

Forward by columns of four, the Pennsylvania 49th marched up a slope and onto the battlefield. Frank shouted to Charley,

"I've never seen anything like this before!"

Charley only half heard what Frank shouted. He was too busy fighting the nausea that rose up in his throat. Scattered all around the fighting men and lying in the pitted field were mangled bodies, arms, legs, swords, horses in grotesque positions. The stench rose into the air with the smoke of battle. The sounds were deafening.

"Steady, lads! Steady beat!" Charley heard O'Toole's shout from somewhere near him. He shut his eyes for a second and beat his drum harder, concentrating only on its reassuring rhythm.

"Double quick, 49th!"

The men marched into battle to the direct aid of two of General Sumner's batteries which were pinned down by enemy fire. In spite of his fear, Charley felt pride well up in his chest as the battle-weary troops of the 43rd New York loudly cheered their arrival. Pressing forward, the Pennsylvania 49th repulsed the Rebel skirmishers who were on the verge of capturing the Union artillery.

"Forward men and to your left!"

Charley heard the command from behind him and turned to see the yellow-haired major sitting astride his horse with pistol raised above his head, urging the regiment forward. A shell whizzed low overhead, and Charley threw himself to the ground. When he was able to resume his drumming, Charley glanced over his shoulder to see that the major had retreated to the safety of the woods.

The 49th formed a defensive line facing the west woods. The rescued artillery batteries moved up at full gallop and wheeled into position opposite the newly deployed Confederate batteries across the open field.

Charley and Frank looked at each other in puzzlement. They had been ordered in at an angle and so close to the artillery they realized that when their regiment opened fire on the enemy, they would be firing through their own men! All the men recognized this, but, without the command of an officer, they were hesitant to change position. Everyone remained in uncertainty until General Hancock himself rode up in front.

"Men, who put you here?" General Hancock demanded.

Charley watched as the general reined in his horse. The animal's head was held high and its nostrils flared as it pranced nervously.

"Our major, sir," the soldiers replied.

"Where is your major?" General Hancock was clearly enraged.

"Behind that large oak tree at the edge of the woods, sir."

"Tell your major to come here, instantly!" ordered General Hancock. His face looked like thunder as he awaited the appearance of the major.

In spite of the noise and danger surrounding them, Charley grinned when he heard Frank say, "That tree is big enough to hide old yellow hair, his shiny boots, and horse, too."

They watched as the major appeared cautiously from behind the oak. Hat set at an angle, yellow hair falling over blue coated shoulders, and brass buttons shining, he rode up and saluted the general.

"Do you want your men all cut to pieces? What do you mean?" the general shouted at the disconcerted major, embarrassing him before the men of his regiment.

Before the flustered major could answer, an aide galloped up to General Hancock and interrupted, "Come away from here, sir. You ought not to be here. The enemy is coming right toward us!"

"Let them come," Hancock replied. "That's what we are here for." Then, turning to the regiment, he gave the direct order, "Step back, men, step back!"

The column of men swung back out of the line of friendly fire.

"Now men, stay there until you are ordered away. This place must be held at all hazards!" Taking a flask from his pocket, General Hancock took a long drink. Ignoring the major, he turned to the artillery captain and said, "Now, Captain, let them have it!"

Charley expected at any moment to see the general fall dead from his horse, but he rode away unharmed through shot and shell.

They opened fire upon the enemy. Charley was not used to being so near to the artillery batteries, and this new thunder was deafening. Enemy in the field before him dropped like flies to the ground, and he could see some, who were wounded, crawling back toward the woods from which they came. Charley looked to his right and saw both Patrick and Hans standing white-faced and as stunned as he was. An explosion in front of him threw bits of earth and rocks up into his face, and he flung himself to the vibrating ground, covering his eyes. He felt a tug from behind and turned to see Sergeant O'Toole motioning him back. Charley, Frank, and Hans slowly and deliberately, bent low, and encumbered by their drums, made their way back toward the east woods. Shot and shell swept low over them like blasts of wind. They moved in what seemed an endless progress toward safety. Charley saw a cannon ball crash into an oak tree ahead of him, impaling itself in the large trunk and dislodging the major and his horse from their hiding place. Both man and animal hastily scrambled deeper into the woods.

A moment later, a sudden jolt thrust Old Betsy into Charley's side and threw him forward against Frank. Frank caught him and eased him to the ground. Charley touched the split frame of the drum, and then felt his body underneath. He held his hand up to his face and saw that it was covered with his own warm blood. "I'm hit," he said in amazement.

Charley could see Frank's mouth forming the words "He's hit!" but the thunder of battle obliterated the cry for help.

Suddenly Sergeant O'Toole was there, looming over him.

"Oh, laddie, what have they done ta ya?" he said. Ignoring the whizzing minié balls, he scooped Charley up in his arms and dashed into the cover of the woods. Frank followed, carrying Charley's broken drum.

Chapter Fifteen

Sharpsburg, Maryland —— September 17–20, 1862

Sergeant O'Toole continued at a steady lope with Charley cradled in his arms. He stopped only long enough to ask, "Where is the nearest surgery?" Frank kept up with him, cradling Old Betsy in his arms, his own drum bouncing against his side. His fear of battle was gone, but now a new fear dragged at him. Was he going to lose his friend? His only real friend? He realized suddenly how much Charley's steady, unquestioning friendship had come to mean to him.

"He won't die," Frank said aloud to himself. "He can't." He thrust those thoughts aside and concentrated only on reaching the field hospital. Sweat and grime poured down his face, and he removed the strap of his own bothersome drum, discarding it as he kept pace with O'Toole.

Finally they reached the fenced yard of a farmhouse. A red flag drooped above the door in the heavy, windless air, indicating a hastily-established surgery. Groaning, wounded men lay scattered about the grass and a couple of weary-looking women bent over them.

"Where's the surgeon?" Sergeant O'Toole bellowed as he entered the gate. Frank could hear him breathing heavily. "I have

a lad here. A young lad! He must see a surgeon!" Then, tenderly he looked down at Charley and said. "Are ya hurtin', laddie?"

Charley looked up at him, his eyes large and dark in his white face. He gave a weak smile, but didn't answer.

He looks so small, Frank thought. I know I used to call him a runt, a pip-squeak, but I didn't think he was still so small.

"Just lay him here in the grass, Sergeant," a kindly woman spoke. "I'll see to his wound, and then the surgeon will do what he can."

Ignoring her, he strode through the open door of the house and bellowed again, "Surgeon needed here!" Then softly to Charley, "Easy, Boy O, we'll have ya right as rain in no time." Then again he shouted, "Surgeon! Now!"

Frank placed Old Betsy on the ground outside the door and followed the sergeant in. A tall man approached them. His face was drawn and tired. His shoulders drooped. A blood-stained apron covered the front of him from chin to knees.

The surgeon placed his hand on O'Toole's arm. "Easy, Sergeant. Bring him over here."

"He's only a lad, Doctor," O'Toole said as he gently placed Charley on the table.

Frank and Sergeant O'Toole stepped back as the surgeon's helpers cut Charley's tunic away and tossed it to the floor. Blood ran from a large gash in Charley's side. Frank gasped at the sight of the raw wound, blackened by bits of shrapnel. He fought a wave of nausea.

At the sudden realization of Frank's presence, Sergeant O'Toole placed an arm around Frank's shoulders and pressed him down into a convenient chair against the wall. "Take a deep breath, lad. And keep your eyes away from the blood. Ya've seen worse in your battlefield duties."

Frank managed a nod. But those other wounds were not the wounds of his best and only friend, he thought!

The surgeon and his assistants surrounded the table, blocking Charley from view. Heedlessly they stepped through blood and surgical debris scattered about on the floor. Frank spied Charley's leather pouch in a pool of blood next to the discarded tunic. He inched forward from the chair and bent to retrieve the pouch, but he was not quick enough. Just as he stretched his hand out, a large boot came down upon the pouch and crushed it further into the blood.

"Get away, boy!" the owner of the boot yelled. He shifted his foot, and Frank scooped up the pouch and darted from the close, foul-smelling house into the relatively fresh air of the yard.

Frank grabbed Old Betsy from its spot outside the door and dashed across the yard jumping over wounded men who sprawled on the grass.

"Look out there, soldier!" growled a man, hobbling with a stick, as he fought to stay upright when Frank and Old Betsy nearly crashed into him.

Frank hardly noticed or heard what was around him. His head was filled only with thoughts of his friend, the awful gash of a wound, and the hot pokers he saw glowing ominously on small fires near the surgery. He knew they were used to seal up wounds. He knew that it was necessary to prevent a wounded man from bleeding to death, but . . .

Finally he slumped to the ground and leaned his back against the rough stones of a wall. He wiped the sweat from his face with the sleeve of his filthy tunic. Then he looked at the blood-stained leather pouch. It was still wet, and Frank rubbed it against the dry grass at his feet. He loosened the drawstring and removed a well-worn folded paper. He could not read the graceful script, but he knew it spelled Elspeth Sinclair's name and address. Finally, he took from the pouch the lock of golden hair, carefully tied with a sky-blue ribbon. Such beautiful hair, he thought. Gently he replaced the lock of hair and the folded paper. Drawing the pouch tight, he tucked it safely into his pocket.

Reaching to his side, he picked up Old Betsy. Her rim was split, and the skin of the top was gashed open. He tried to smooth the skin back into place, but it would not stay. Harder now he pushed the sides together. Becoming desperate, he did not notice his fingers bleeding from the splintered wood. Tears ran down his cheeks. He was sobbing aloud, but he did not notice. If only he could fix Old Betsy, make her well again, then Charley could get well again!

"Leave off, lad. Can ya not see it's beyond repair?"

Frank looked up to see Sergeant O'Toole standing over him. He stared at the sergeant, afraid to ask aloud about Charley. But O'Toole must have read the unspoken question on his face because, nodding his head back toward the makeshift hospital, he said, "Sure, he's in good hands now. We'll be back to see him soon. Up now, lad, and back ta the regiment."

Frank stood up wearily, still holding Old Betsy.

"There's no use in takin' that broken drum back with ya, lad. As I said, it's beyond salvation."

But Frank held on to it stubbornly, set his jaw, and defiantly looked O'Toole in the eye.

O'Toole looked back at him for a second and then merely nodded. They trudged slowly back toward the sound of the battle.

That evening, the cannons now silent, Frank, Hans, and Patrick carried out their grim duty of clearing the cornfield of the wounded and dead. More and more field hospitals had sprung up, but as often as they could, the boys made their way back to the farmhouse where Charley lay on the narrow cot. A pile of arms and legs, most with sleeves or trousers and boots still on them, grew outside the kitchen door. The ground was a slippery, dark reddish brown from the spilled blood of all the wounded. Frank stepped inside the open door and found Charley in what used to be the parlor. He lay small and still under a light blanket, his eyes closed, but his face calm. A nurse saw Frank and said, "He's sleeping peacefully. No need to disturb him now."

Frank took another look at him and went back out into the dark night. The next trip Patrick went inside, and the next, Hans. But each time Charley was asleep.

September 18, 1862

Before dawn, Frank headed once more back to the farmhouse. He was afraid at any moment the regiment would be called back into battle or even put on the road again. He remembered how it had been during the Seven Days' Battles. Now lanterns pierced the darkness as the dead and wounded were still being removed from the battlefields all around. A single light flickered low in the room where many more cots now lined the walls. Some men moaned softly. Frank strained to see the forms. "Charley. Charley King," he hissed in a low voice.

"Over here, Frank." The voice trailed off into a whisper, "here."

He followed the sound to the opposite corner where the cot had been moved. He put his lantern on the floor near the bed. "Charley," he whispered. "You look so . . ." He had been about to say small, but thought better of it.

Charley managed a weak smile. "Can you tell my father and mother I'm hurt? They'll come and bring me home."

"Sure, Captain Sweeney is takin' care of all that. He'll send a telegram. Here, this fell out of your pocket, but I got it back for you." Frank held out the small leather pouch.

"Elspeth," Charley sighed her name. "Will you write her for me, Frank?"

"You'll write her your own self in a week or so," said Frank. "I got Old Betsy. She was hit, but I'll get her fixed up for you," he added.

Charley raised himself up on his elbow and in a low voice spoke intently. "Grandpa Eb was wrong, Frank. He said it was all for honor and glory. That Reb and Yank we found who had stabbed each other through—Was that for Yankee honor and glory or for Rebel honor and glory? Don't fix the drum, Frank. Leave it as it is." Charley turned his face away, breathing heavily, exhausted by the talking.

Frank shifted from one foot to the other, not knowing what to say.

"No more visiting now, young man. Let him rest." A woman had appeared at the bedside so quietly that Frank was startled by her voice.

"I'll come back tonight, Charley." He gently touched his friend's hand which lay motionless on top of the cover, but Charley did not hear. His eyes were closed, and he breathed the regular rhythm of sleep.

As promised, Frank returned that evening, this time with a group from the 49th. Charley really was a favorite of the whole company, Frank thought. They weren't all allowed in at once. The men would have more than filled the entire room. Frank stood next to Sergeant O'Toole and Jacob Adams to be sure he had his turn with them, and finally, after one by one the others trailed out, mostly silent. some shaking their heads, Frank went inside with O'Toole and Jacob.

Charley looked different this time. His face was red and hot, his eyes were glassy and hollow-looking. He was restless, but every slight movement seemed to pain him.

"Sing the song, Jacob," Charley said.

Jacob Adams had to lean his ear close to Charley's mouth to hear him. "The song?" he asked.

"Up in the sky," Charley mumbled.

"Oh yes, that one." Then Jacob sang,

> Oh Mother, how pretty the moon looks tonight;
> 'Twas never so cunning before.
> Its two little arms are so sharp and so bright;
> I hope they won't grow anymore.

> If I were up there with you by my side;
> We'd rock in it nicely you'd see.
> We'd sit in the middle and hold by both ends.
> And on the next rainbow come home.

> We'd call to the stars to keep out of our way;
> Lest we should rock over their toes.

And there we would stay till the end of the day;
And on the next rainbow come home.

Charley closed his eyes and listened as the melody filled the air.

"He's back up in the balloon, flying above all," Frank thought as he watched the peaceful expression settle over his friend's face.

"That was some mighty fine singing, mister," the wounded man on the next cot said. He lay uncovered. His right leg was missing from below the knee. The stump was bound with a bloody bandage. "How about giving us another?"

"Yeah, another, another," other men's voices chimed in.

"Can't sing to a room full of strangers," Jacob replied.

"Well, I'm Tom Cosgrove, New Jersey 1st," said the young man with the bloody stump.

"Quincy Drummond, New York 43rd," said the next man. "My ma used to sing that song to me," he added.

Those who were well enough shouted out their names and regiments. Finally, a whisper struggled to be heard. "Will . . . Will . . ." The men quieted and strained to listen. "William Murphy, New York 69th." A boy of about seventeen, whose eyes were covered by bandages, held his hands out before him, as if to feel the presence of the others. "Can you hear?" His whisper faded.

"We hear you, Billy," Jacob replied softly.

Some men wept openly, others listened, smiling as if dreaming private dreams, as songs of love and home were sung in Jacob's clear baritone voice.

When they left the hospital, Patrick, Hans, and Frank walked silently, followed by Sergeant O'Toole and Jacob. Finally Patrick spoke, "At least Charley's still whole. He's not blind or without an arm or leg like some of those poor fellows."

"Yeah, but I feel scared that Charley is going to die," said Hans. "If it can happen to Charley, it can happen to any of us."

Frank stopped and placed his face up close to Hans'. "Listen, he's goin' to be all right. His pa will come for him and fetch him home, and he'll be all right!"

"Sure," said Hans. "Sure."

Taken back by Frank's intensity, Patrick nodded in agreement. "He'll be fine."

Frank hung behind as Patrick and Hans quickened their pace toward camp. He did not want the others to see the fright in his eyes. He could hear Sergeant O'Toole and Jacob behind him in conversation.

"What manner of men are we to make war on children, Jacob?"

"I don't know, Michael. That poor lad back there will have a hard time, now that infection has set in. Thank God, my Robby is out of it for the duration."

September 19, 1862

On Friday, word spread quickly that General Lee and his Rebs had retreated back across the Potomac into Virginia. McClellan did not order his army to pursue. Throughout the day Frank tried repeatedly to see Charley, but he was turned away by the kindly, but firm, Sisters of Charity who were now tending the wounded.

September 20, 1862

"He needs to know we care, Sergeant," Frank nearly begged O'Toole.

The sergeant with an arm about Frank's shoulders, said, "Come on, lad. We'll pay him a visit. They'll let ya in with me."

Frank watched from the foot of the bed while Charley tossed feverishly on the soaked sheets. A small dark-haired woman seated next to him dipped a rag in a bowl of water, wrung it tightly, and then laid it across his brow, all the while murmuring softly to him. The hem of her full skirt lay in folds against the floor. It was stained a dark, ugly red from the blood she had waded through.

Charley flung his arm up and knocked the rag from his head. The woman calmly replaced it. "Mama, Mama," Charley moaned.

"I am here, son," the woman answered, taking the hand Charley had so fervently extended.

"Mama," he repeated in wonder. "You came." He opened his eyes, focusing on her.

"Yes, son," she said.

But you're not his mother! Frank wanted to shout. He wanted to grab Charley by the shoulders and shake him into reality! Instead, he squeezed his knuckles until they were white. His fingernails dug into the palms of his hands, and he was conscious of Sergeant O'Toole's tight grip on his shoulder as if to hold him back.

"Mama, I can smell the lilacs in our garden. But it's getting dark, now. Did Lewis light the lamps in Papa's shop?" he whispered.

"Yes, Charley. They are all lit," she said.

"Mama, Grandpa Eb is here. Do you see? He wants me to come with him." In a burst of energy Charley raised his head from the pillow. The nurse supported his shoulders. Eyes opened wide, but unseeing, he shouted, "Ma." Then in a whisper, "Oh Mama, it hurts. I'm so tired."

Frank could stand no more. He ducked his head under the sergeant's arm which still rested on his shoulder and darted from the room. He did not see the dark-haired woman gently place her hand over Charley's eyes to close them or O'Toole cross himself and bow his head in silent prayer.

Outside, Frank started to run, slowly at first, then faster and faster. He tried to run from the smell of sickness and death, but it was of no use. The stench was in the air which filled his lungs. Panting, he stopped by the side of the road which led into camp. Boonsboro Pike was filled with traffic; supply wagons, civilian carriages and wagons taking wounded and dead home at last, medical wagons moving wounded to hospitals in Frederick or in Washington.

Frank spoke to a soldier on picket duty. "Anyone asked for directions to the Pennsylvania 49th wounded?"

"Son, so many people are lookin' for so many other people, it'll be a wonder if anybody's left to fight this here war," the grizzled veteran replied.

"Well, this is a man name of Pennell King, lookin' for his boy. When he comes, tell him Charley's in the hospital yonder."

"Listen, son," the soldier began.

Frank thrust his chin forward and clenched his fists. The man looked at him and then spoke more calmly. "All right, I'll tell him when he comes."

At twilight Frank stood frozen staring at the empty cot, un-believing. "No . . .!" a silent scream filled his head, his whole being. He looked frantically around at the other cots, the other soldiers. "Charley," he said. Then, "Charley King! Charley King!" louder and louder.

"He's dead," said Tom, the young man in the next bed. He struggled to push himself up, his useless stump of a leg not al-lowing him to stand. "You were here. I thought you knew."

"No, no! He's not dead. Charley, Charley King," Frank shouted as he continued to search among the wounded for his friend.

"Sister!" someone called. "We need help here."

Two nurses came forward and tried to calm him, but Frank shook them off. The small dark-haired woman who had com-forted Charley appeared.

"What is all this commotion?" she asked.

"You're the one who said you were his mama. You lied to him," Frank blurted out. "Where is he?"

"Young man, this is Miss Clara Barton you are speaking to. Please show some respect," one of the nurses said.

"It's all right, sister. Thank you." Miss Barton led Frank away from the patients into the back of the house. He sat quietly now.

He had no more energy to resist. He knew before she spoke that his friend was dead. He had known all along. She handed him a tin cup filled with water. He stared at it. She gently guided his hand up to his mouth, and he drank automatically, not tasting. All the while she was speaking softly to him.

". . . so you see, I did not lie, but only comforted a dying boy who wished for his mama."

There it was again . . . dying, dead, dead.

"It's because I couldn't fix Old Betsy," Frank spoke to himself.

The woman looked at him, puzzled. Then she said, "Rest here as long as you please. There are many others like your friend whom I must attend . . . so many others."

Eventually he rose from the chair and made his way back to camp.

September 21, 1862

A somber Pennell King stood next to his wagon, head bowed, as six men of the Pennsylvania 49th placed his son's pine coffin in the open bed. Earlier, Frank had seen Mr. King as he drove his wagon into camp. He was an average sized man, with a neatly trimmed dark beard, broad brimmed hat, dark suit coat removed and neatly folded on the back of the wagon seat, white shirt sleeves rolled to the elbow because of the warm Maryland afternoon. On the side of the wagon was printed in gold letters, KING'S TAILORING, FINE TAILORING FOR GENTLEMEN, WEST CHESTER, PENNSYLVANIA.

Now all of Company F stood at attention behind the wagon while a lone bugler played the haunting melody of "Taps." They saluted, then slowly, silently the company dispersed, all except Frank, Jacob Adams, and Sergeant O'Toole.

"Here are Charley's belongings, sir," Frank said as he held out the leather pouch, Grandpa Eb's knife, and the broken drum. "He wanted Lewis to have the whittling knife," he added.

Pennell King looked at Frank, puzzled. "Why, you can give it yourself to Lewis. We have unfinished business to be taken care of. Remember our agreement with Charles?"

Frank's eyes widened. He felt his heart beat faster. He looked first at Mr. King, not quite understanding what he had just heard. "Do you mean . . .?" He did not finish the question, but Pennell King answered, "You're part of our family now, son. It would still be Charley's wish."

Frank looked at Sergeant O'Toole, who suddenly became very busy inspecting the wagon wheel. Jacob also was engrossed with examining the toe of his own boot. Finally O'Toole's eyes met Frank's. The sergeant gave the slightest of nods and turned away.

Frank needed no more encouragement. With tears in his eyes and without a word he climbed up on the wagon seat next to Pennell King and placed the broken drum on the seat between them.

The challenge to Frank came from the posted sentry as the wagon started down the dusty road ladened with its sad cargo. "Soldier, where do you think you're going? Have you filled your enlistment? How long have you been in?"

Pennell King did not stop, but proceeded at a steady pace. Frank's stomach flipped over, but before he could reply, he heard Sergeant O'Toole's strong voice answer for him, "Four seasons and a hundred years."